DOLPHIN IN THE DEEP

A  ...es is a dream come true for ...imal-lover Mandy Hope. She can't wait to meet the animals that live there! Mandy spends a lot of time at the local dolphinarium, playing with two tame dolphins, Bob and Bing. The dolphins are happy performing together—but when Bob dies, the lonely Bing pines for company. Mandy and her friend Joel are worried about his future—until they come up with a daring plan . . . But will it work?

ANIMAL ARK: DOLPHIN IN THE DEEP

Lucy Daniels

Galaxy

CHIVERS PRESS
BATH

First published 1998
by
Hodder Children's Books
This Large Print edition published by
Chivers Press
by arrangement with
Hodder Children's Books
2000

ISBN 0 7540 6137 X

British Library Cataloguing in Publication Data

Daniels, Lucy
Dolphin in the deep—Large print ed.—(Animal Ark.
In America)
1. Animal Ark (Imaginary place)—Juvenile
fiction 2. Dolphins—Juvenile fiction
3. Children's stories 4. Large type books
I. Title
823. 9'14[J]

ISBN 0-7540-6137-X

Printed and bound in Great Britain by
REDWOOD BOOKS, Trowbridge, Wiltshire

Special thanks to Jenny Oldfield.
Thanks also to C.J. Hall, B.Vet.Med.,
M.R.C.V.S., for reviewing the
veterinary information contained in
this book.

CHAPTER ONE

'You know something? Right this minute I could be sitting watching a movie in a plane over the ocean!' Joel Logan sighed. He'd turned down a chance to fly with his grandmother to England.

Mandy Hope lay back, her arms behind her head, as their boat bobbed on a clear blue sea. 'Tough. Instead, you're stuck here in paradise.'

'Nothing to do, nowhere to go,' Joel moaned. He dipped his toe in the water. 'I must be crazy.'

'Why didn't you go, then?' Mandy rolled over on to her stomach. The deck of the boat was warm from the sun, the waves sparkled and danced. In the distance, she could see the tiny town of Dixie Springs perched at the edge of the bay.

''Cos . . .' He sat at the front of the launch, waiting for his grandfather, Jerry Logan, to start up the engine. They were drifting under the high sun,

1

with not another boat in sight.

'Because you happen to like it here,' Mandy teased. 'Only it wouldn't be cool to admit you were having a good time.' That was how Joel was; pretending not to be interested in things like sponge fishing, which was what they were doing now.

'No way. It was 'cos I had to stay and look after Grandpa, keep him out of trouble,' Joel insisted. He perched on the edge of the boat, baseball cap pulled low over his tanned face.

'Yeah, sure.' His grandfather put down his pair of binoculars and took the wheel. 'And I had to stay home in Blue Bayous to take care of folks' gardens. Life's real hard.' He grinned as he choked the boat's engine back into life. 'Digging, weeding, planting, watering . . .' Though he was past seventy, Jerry Logan still ran Green Earth Gardens, his small gardening business. 'Guys my age should be taking things easy,' he joked.

'And I couldn't go back home with Gran and Grandad because you two needed someone to keep you both out of trouble!' Mandy joined in the joke. 'Tough decision.' She sighed and sat up, staring down into the deep blue water.

'Yeah, you could have been watching a movie with me, miles above the Atlantic.'

'Instead of messing about in Florida for an extra few weeks.'

'Back to British weather,' Jerry Logan reminded her.

'. . . Rain,' she agreed.

'Back to work,' Jerry added.

'. . . Helping out at Animal Ark for the rest of the summer holidays.' Cleaning cages, making appointments, visiting patients in the Yorkshire village of Welford with her parents, the local vets. Suddenly the joke went flat. Mandy had to admit that she did miss her mum and dad, and life at Animal Ark.

But she'd chosen to stay on when her grandparents flew home to Welford with Bee Logan. There was so much to do and see here in America, Mandy would have been mad to turn down the offer to stay longer.

3

'OK, time to head for home,' Jerry Logan decided. He choked the outboard motor back into life.

'But we didn't see any live sponges yet,' Joel complained.

Mandy had seen hundreds of them set out to dry on the harbourside at Dixie Springs. From a distance they looked like rows of brown coconuts or curled-up hedgehogs. Close to, you could see the delicate structure of the sponges.

''Cos you didn't dive to find them yet.' The easygoing old man didn't mind one way or the other. He steered the boat in a slow semi-circle to point towards the shore. 'Do you wanna do that now?'

Joel shrugged.

'Well, do you?' He turned to Mandy.

'Just to take a look. But how deep do we have to dive?'

'Until you get to the bottom,' he grinned.

'Are there lots?' She leaned over again to gaze down into the clear depths.

'Sure. Lucky for the divers, we don't

4

allow tuna nets off Blue Bayous. That means all marine life gets protected. There's plenty of everything.' He explained how the big, commercial nets were illegal. 'Lucky for the dolphins too. If the waters get over-fished, there's nothing for them to eat.'

'Dolphins?' Mandy pricked up her ears. Dolphins sounded more interesting than sponges. Anything that breathed and moved, in or out of the water, was better than sponges as far as she was concerned.

'Yep, Dixie Springs is a good bay for them. They seem to like it.'

'How come?' Mandy knew the sea off the southwest coast of Florida was popular with bottlenose dolphins. But why especially Dixie Springs?

'They like the warm water,' Jerry explained.

'Me too. Let's go take a look.' Joel lifted his feet clear of the water and the boat set off.

'And in this bay they can do a spot of team fishing. See, they form a line and herd the fish towards the shore. Then they pick them off one by one.

'Pretty clever.' Mandy was impressed. She scanned the waves for sleek grey shapes.

'Mostly at dawn and dusk,' Joel's grandpa continued. 'But I guess we could get lucky.'

It was midday. The sun glared overhead as the white boat cut through the blue sea.

'Over there!' Joel stood up and pointed.

'Where?' Mandy shot across to his side of the boat.

'Not there. There.' He pointed in a new direction.

'Where?' She concentrated so hard she almost fell over the side.

'Just kidding.' Joel grinned and swung under the silver rail into the tiny cabin. This was one of his favourite tricks.

'Do they really fish as a team?' Mandy had learned to ignore Joel's practical jokes.

'Yep, they're that smart.' Jerry Logan cruised across the bay. 'I've seen them doing it.' In his checked shirt, with his short grey hair and silver-

6

rimmed glasses, he looked happy and relaxed.

In spite of the fact that Joel had tricked her, Mandy still kept her eyes peeled for dolphins. She was looking for their grey submarine shapes playing among the white spray made by their boat, or leaping out of the water ahead of them.

'What was that?' she said suddenly, craning over the edge. 'Joel, come and look.'

'Yeah, like I'm that stupid!' He sank into the seat in the shade of the canopy, refusing to budge.

'No, really. I think I saw something.'

'It's called the ocean.' Joel lay back, feet up, cap over his eyes.

'Yes, I did. There it is again!' She was sure this time. 'Slow down, Jerry. I can see two of them. Three, four!' They were shadows swimming up to the boat, deep underwater, twisting this way and that.

Hearing the note of excitement in her voice, Jerry Logan shut down the engine and let the boat drift.

Mandy leaned right out. '. . . Five,

six! Honestly, Joel, you're mad to miss this!'

The sleek grey shapes were rising closer to the surface. They'd seen the boat and were coming to investigate. Now one was only a few metres away. Mandy could make out his fins, the strong up and down movement of his tail.

Joel snored, pretending to fall asleep.

'You should see him! He's over two metres long. And he's got this big round forehead and a long nose like a beak. I know this sounds silly, but it looks as if he's smiling at me!'

The dolphin poked his face up against the hull of the boat, then he turned on his back to show Mandy his pale belly. He scudded gently with his flippers, doing an easy backstroke.

'Yeah, yeah, yeah!' Joel opened one eye and peered out from under his cap.

'Here comes another one. It's much smaller. Maybe it's a baby!'

The young one was lively. He twisted under the boat, disappeared and then came tumbling back into view. His back

8

fin broke the surface for a second, then vanished.

'Did you see that?' Mandy called.

'All I see is you making a fool of yourself.' Joel wasn't going to let Mandy get her own back. She could tell him there were *twenty* dolphins swimming around the boat and he still wouldn't move a muscle.

'OK, if you don't believe me, watch this!' She'd seen another playful dolphin join the first youngster and had an idea about what they planned to do next.

As Joel peered out from under his cap, the dolphins began to surge through the water towards the boat. Mandy held her breath. Their fins thrust towards the surface, launching them out of the water in a burst of white spray.

Their bodies arched clear, then flipped sideways; one to the right, one to the left. A split second, and they were gone.

'Wow!' Joel jumped out of his seat. 'Did you see that? Two of them. They were *this* close!' He scrambled so fast to the side of the boat that he made it rock. 'What did I tell you? Didn't I say there were hundreds of dolphins in this bay?'

Jerry Logan glanced at Mandy and winked. 'Here come three more. They're real friendly. See that one giving the small guy a slap with her tail? She's keeping him in line. I guess she's the mother!'

Mandy grinned. It wasn't Joel changing his mind that was so funny. It was the sight of the dolphins. Everything about them; every flick of their tails, every glimpse of their curious smiling faces made her want to laugh and jump in the water to join them.

'It's a whole pod—a school of them.' Jerry too was enjoying the sight. 'Some of these youngsters are only a couple of months old, but they sure can move.

'How fast?' She hung far out over the side, tipping the small boat.

'Around 30 miles per hour. I've seen them do more.' He'd lived all his life in Florida, except for the years he'd spent in England as a soldier. That was when he'd met Bee, married her and whisked her back to Blue Bayous. They'd raised a family here, and now every summer their grandson, Joel, came from New York to stay with them.

Mandy gasped as three more dolphins sped towards the boat. They dipped at the last minute and swam underneath, rising to the surface in a shower of sea spray. They poked their pointed noses at the boat and made gentle creaking noises.

'They're talking to you,' Jerry grinned. 'Try talking back.'

'How?' Mandy reached out to try to touch the nearest dolphin, but he flipped backwards out of reach.

'They like this kind of noise.' Jerry tapped the metal rail that Mandy was leaning against. 'It makes them curious.'

She tried it gently, tapping softly with her fingernails.

'Louder.'

Tap-tap-tap. She rattled her nails against the metal.

And all the dolphins came swimming up, swirling to the surface, making their own strange creaking noises, blowing hard through the blowholes on the tops of their heads. There were more than a dozen, rising and listening, chattering out an answer to the new sound.

'You can train these guys,' Joel told her, coming quietly alongside. 'They use a whistle to teach them tricks. I've seen it in the zoo.'

She shook her head. 'I don't think I'd like that.'

'How come?'

'Dunno. It sounds a bit cruel.' She never liked to see wild animals being tamed and taught to do cheap stunts.

'They like it. It's fun.' Joel shrugged and swung his legs and body under the rail.

'What are you doing?' Mandy was afraid Joel would scare the wonderful dolphins away.

'Going swimming. You coming?'

She glanced at Jerry, who nodded. 'No problem. I'll stick around until you're ready to leave,' he promised. He glanced up at the sun and chose a shady spot under the canopy.

By now Joel had lowered himself into the water and the dolphins were keeping their distance, checking out the new arrival.

'Can we?' Mandy asked, hardly able to believe their luck.

'Sure. They won't hurt you.' Jerry smiled and nodded. 'There's never been a single recorded case of a dolphin making an unprovoked attack on a human being, and you're not about to be the first!'

'It's not that!' Mandy held her breath as she poised, ready to follow him.

Joel struck out, clear of the boat. 'They can kill a shark,' he yelled. 'They ram him in the side: *whack*!'

Mandy narrowed her eyes, looking for a clear space in the blue water. When she found one, she made a neat dive. Then she was in the sea, slicing through the water. Mandy dived under the surface, and felt the cool water welcome her. At last she opened her eyes—and found herself face to face with one of nature's most brilliant creatures.

The dolphin nosed against her,

nudging her gently. His beak was hard and his small eyes stared curiously.

Under the water Mandy stretched out her hand. The dolphin's head was smooth and firm, and when he rolled on to his back to let her stroke his belly, she felt the powerful muscles that propelled his body through the water. He curved his fins and rolled again, twisting upwards towards the sunlight.

Still holding her breath, she followed him. She kicked and broke the surface, drawing air into her lungs.

Nearby, Joel used a bold, noisy crawl to come up alongside two of the bigger dolphins who cruised side by side.

'Watch this!' he yelled. He made a lunge at the nearest dolphin. 'I'm hitching a ride!'

Mandy grinned as the dolphin slipped neatly out of reach. 'I don't think so!'

But Joel was persistent and the dolphins were good-tempered. They let him lunge again, waiting until he came up between them and managed to fling his arm round one of them. Then the dolphin set off across the bay, towing

Joel in her wake.

'Yeah!' Joel yelled at the top of his voice. Spray rose and shone in all the colours of the rainbow. It was better than the water rides in any theme park; faster, more daring, just fabulous!

Mandy looked on enviously.

But the dolphin who was towing Joel had a fine sense of humour. She took the boy far out to sea. She let him yell and shout and enjoy the trip. Then she dumped him. She came to a sudden stop and dived.

'Hey!' Joel had to let go. His yell turned to a wail. He was stranded a great distance from anywhere, paddling helplessly in the deep blue sea.

Jerry Logan grinned and started the motor. 'Jump aboard,' he told Mandy, leaning out to lend her a hand. 'We gotta sail to the rescue!'

And the school of dolphins came with them, making for the forward end of the boat, crisscrossing their bow wave, weaving from side to side.

Mandy sat on the deck, her fair hair dripping down her back, watching the dolphins play. *Trust Joel*, she thought.

Showing off, then getting dumped.

He yelled for them to hurry. 'What took you so long?' he asked as his grandfather cut the engine and bobbed alongside.

The dolphins had formed a circle around the noisy, stranded boy. They seemed to grin as they opened their jaws and took in big mouthfuls of water.

'Uh-oh!' Jerry Logan warned. 'Watch out!'

Too late. The dolphins had Joel surrounded. They aimed and fired.

Half a dozen of the most playful ones were getting their own back as they squirted water at him. The jets rose like fountains and sprayed him from all directions. He disappeared beneath a torrent of sparkling drops.

'Gotcha!' Mandy grinned. Sometimes Joel deserved everything he got!

CHAPTER TWO

'Have I ever rescued a dolphin?' Lauren Young repeated Mandy's question.

It was the day after the visit to Dixie Springs. Mandy and Joel had gone to help out at the rescue centre in the north of the island. GRROWL, or the Group for the Rescue and Rehabilitation of Wild Life, was run by Lauren, who was a qualified vet, together with a band of volunteers. They took in sick and wounded animals, nursed them back to health and tried to release them into their natural habitat.

'Yes. I mean, if there was a sick dolphin washed up on the shore, would you be able to look after it?' Mandy knew that Lauren cared for racoons and squirrels, pelicans and turtles, deer and alligators. Everything that lived on Blue Bayous could find shelter here.

'That's a hard one.' Lauren examined an eagle's broken wing in one of the large cages in the yard of the rescue centre. The bird's head and tail were pure white, while its body and wings were dark. The eagle turned its head to peck at Lauren's hand with its hooked beak as she spread its mighty wing. But she held it expertly from behind, keeping out of harm's way.

'Why? Because they live in salt water?' The rescue centre was in the middle of a huge wilderness area with natural lakes and swamps, but Mandy didn't think a dolphin would be able to survive in the stagnant, brackish water.

'Yep. We'd need a special tank. If we heard about a dolphin getting sick, we'd probably call in a marine expert. We wouldn't treat it ourselves.' Lauren worked quickly to put the eagle back on its perch. Then she and Mandy stepped outside the cage.

The huge bird ruffled its feathers and poked its head in warning. It fixed them with its beady eyes.

Lauren, a young, slim woman with curly black hair, who reminded Mandy of her mum, turned to her. 'Why do you ask?'

'No reason.' Mandy went ahead, taking a bucket of fish to the cage of brown pelicans. Helping Lauren was one of the high points of her holiday here on Blue Bayous. Wall-to-wall sunshine, white beaches, blue seas and GRROWL. What could be better?

The ungainly pelicans waddled towards her, the slack pouches under their long beaks wobbling as they walked. They opened their mouths for food.

Mandy picked out a fish by its tail and flung it to the birds. Snap! The nearest pelican snaffled the prize.

Lauren stood outside the cage, arms folded. 'Joel tells me you went swimming with the dolphins yesterday.'

Mandy swung another fish and threw it. 'Did he tell you what they did to him?' She described the drenching Joel had brought on himself.

'I guess he forgot that part.' Lauren laughed. 'Never underestimate a dolphin, hey, Joel!'

Mandy emptied the bucket and turned to see him standing there, his face red. He'd brought Duchess,

Lauren's Great Dane, down into the yard from the first-floor veranda.

'At least I hitched a ride before they got me.' It was more than Mandy had done.

'Call it their sense of fun.' Lauren patted the dog's head. 'I'd be kind of proud if it had happened to me. It means they like you.' She led them on to the racoon enclosure. 'You get other smart animals, like these little guys here, but for me a dolphin is unique.'

Mandy stared through the wire netting at a small group of racoons clinging to a stout tree branch. Their bandit faces peered back, their black hands grasped the branch and their striped tails swung to and fro. They were bright-eyed and alert.

'So what makes dolphins special?' Mandy asked. She realised how happy they made her feel when they surged towards her, but she wanted more hard facts.

'One; the dolphin is the only marine species to move its tail up and down instead of from side to side.' Lauren held up her forefinger and began to list the points. 'Two; they're known to have advanced forms of social behaviour.'

Joel made a dumb face. 'Huh?'

'They take care of one another. For instance, when a baby is born in April, a second female acts as midwife to the mother. She helps the calf to the surface so it can take its first breath, and she'll chase away any nearby sharks.'

'What else?' Mandy urged.

'Three; a dolphin's brain is larger than any other marine mammal's. In fact, it's the same size as a man's.'

'So they think like us? They're as smart as us?' Joel looked doubtful.

'Who knows?' Lauren shrugged. 'How do you measure intelligence? Some scientists will say a dolphin is only as smart as a dog or a chimp. Some say, no way; a dolphin is equal to a man any day.'

'Easily!' Mandy sighed. 'Only, how do you prove it?'

Lauren invited them upstairs for a sandwich and a cold drink. They were still talking dolphins half an hour later, sitting in the shade of the veranda on the cane chairs, waiting for Jerry Logan to call by and take them home.

'I heard a story once,' Lauren told them, 'about a young guy in a fishing boat way out in the Gulf of Mexico.'

Mandy eased back in her seat to listen, keeping one eye closed against the sun's glare, her feet resting idly on Duchess's broad back.

'The boat gets hit by a freak storm and turns over. The fisherman manages to cling to the hull, but there's no way he thinks anyone will come to rescue him. He knows the sharks will be around before too long. He spends a whole night out there, listening to things splashing in the black water all around. Sharks. It's only a matter of time . . .'

Mandy and Joel turned to Lauren, dreading the end.

'But the sun comes up and he sees it's not sharks making the splashes, it's dolphins. And they're doing it to keep the sharks away. He can see the man-eaters' fins slicing through the water, but they can't get at him because of the dolphins. Two days and two nights this goes on. He's dying out there from heat exhaustion. But the dolphins come right up to him and splash him to keep him awake. If he passes out, he'll slip into the water and the sharks will tear him to pieces.'

'What happened? Did they save him?' Joel asked.

'They sprayed him with water and waited until a boat arrived in the nick of time. He lived to tell the tale.'

'Do you believe that?' Joel wanted to know.

Lauren smiled and nodded. 'That man was my pa,' she confided.

Mandy sighed. She thought the story was mysterious and wonderful. 'It's kind of magic!'

'A miracle.' Lauren told them that if it hadn't been for the dolphins, she wouldn't be here now. 'My pa was twenty. He's nearly sixty now, but he still wears a chain round his neck with a gold charm in the shape of a dolphin. He swears he'll never take it off until he dies.'

In the silence that followed, Lauren shook herself and stood up, ready to go back to work. Duchess rose to her feet and plodded indoors.

'What are you thinking?' Joel asked Mandy. Even he had been impressed.

She squinted down at the yard. 'I'm thinking that blue herons and brown pelicans and bald eagles are all very well,' she told him. 'I'm still mad about racoons and crazy about alligators . . .'

'But?'

'. . . It's dolphins from now on!' Dolphins in her dreams, gliding through turquoise water, diving to the coral reefs on the sea bed. Dolphins in the deep.

*   *   *

'How about meeting me at the rescue centre in half an hour?' A few days later, Lauren rang Mandy and issued an invite. 'Something came up. I have to drive to Ibis Gardens.'

'And you want us to come?' Mandy lolled at the kitchen table at Pelican's Roost, munching a cookie. Joel was next door at Moonshadow, swimming in the pool with Courtney Miller. It was a Saturday, five days after Gran and Grandad had flown back to England.

'Sure, if you'd like to. I'm taking Mitch back to Mel Hartley.'

'Who's Mitch?'

'A sea otter. Mel brought him to GRROWL a couple of days ago with a cut leg. He's fine now, though.'

'Hmm.' Sea otters were cute, but Mandy had promised Joel that she would join him and Courtney for a barbecue by the pool. Mrs Miller would be cooking right now. 'I don't know if I can.'

'OK, no problem.' Lauren was about to hang up. 'Some other time.'

'Ibis Gardens?' It was a theme park where there were all kinds of exotic animals: elephants, zebra and giraffe. Not so much a zoo as an 'African experience'. Mandy was tempted. 'Could we call in on Allie?'

Allie was an alligator who couldn't be trusted to be released into the wild since unwise tourists had fed him and turned him into a dangerous manhunter. So they'd had to take him from GRROWL to live in a compound in Ibis Gardens. Mandy was keen to find out how he was getting on in his new home.

'Sure. Yes or no, Mandy? I have to hit the road.'

'Yes!' Mandy promised to get there double quick. She ran next door to find that the barbecue was off after all because Courtney had remembered a dentist's appointment.

So Joel jumped at the chance to come too, and they took a lift from Mrs Miller. She said they had to drive past the rescue centre to keep her daughter's appointment.

'Sure you don't want to take my place at the dentist's?' Courtney grinned at Mandy as she climbed awkwardly out of the car. Her broken leg was still in plaster from an accident a few weeks before.

'Somehow I think he'd spot the difference!' Courtney had fair hair like Mandy, but the similarity ended there. She was tall and tanned and twice as glamorous.

'Have a good day!' Louise Miller called as she waved and drove off.

Mandy and Joel found Lauren in the yard, loading a small cage into the truck. She waved. 'Hi. Mitch would say hi too, but he's kind of upset. He doesn't like being locked up! I've had to take care of him here at GRROWL because the regular Ibis Gardens vet is on vacation.'

Mandy and Joel climbed in the back of the truck and peeped into the cage at the little sea otter. His blunt nose and whiskered face peered back. He had a thick brown coat and webbed feet; his broad tail thumped the floor of the cage.

'Hang on, we'll soon have you back home,' Mandy promised. They had a half-hour drive to the northern tip of the island. 'Does he have his own pool?' she called to Lauren, climbing into the driver's seat.

'No. He shares it.'

'Who with? More otters?'

'Nope. Mitch is the only one.' Lauren backed the truck out of the yard on to the rough track. Then she drove out on to the road.

'Who then?' Mitch was probably

friendly and easy to get on with, except when he was sulking inside a cage.

'Bob and Bing.' Lauren relaxed. She rolled down the window and leaned an elbow against the door. They were on their way, past rows of sea grape trees, across narrow wooden bridges that crossed flat, swampy streams. As always, the sun shone in a deep blue sky. 'This breeze is great,' she sighed.

'Who are Bob and Bing?' Mandy asked. The names were new to her. 'Are they sea lions?' Who could Mitch possibly share a pool with?

Lauren shook her head. 'No. Didn't I say?' Her voice teased, as she glanced in her overhead mirror at the two curious faces in the back. 'Bob and Bing are a major attraction at Ibis Gardens. They're a couple of bottlenose dolphins!'

*   *   *

'Mandy, Joel, meet Bob and Bing.' The dolphin trainer, Mel Hartley, introduced his star duo. He stood at the side of the training pool with Mitch

28

perched happily on his shoulder.

Mandy stared down into the green water, her heartbeat quickening as the two dolphins swam towards them. They came right under her nose, bobbing up with their heads tilted back, their beaks clapping together to make a hard rattling noise.

'They're saying hi!' Mel told them.

'Hi, Bob. Hi, Bing.' Joel knelt by the pool. 'Can we touch them?'

'Sure.' Mel wanted to talk to Lauren about Mitch, so he strolled away across the tiled poolside.

For a few seconds Mandy stood and watched. 'Which is which?' she wondered. To her, the two dolphins looked exactly alike, with their domed grey foreheads, small eyes set well back on the side of their heads, and their wide, smiling mouths.

'Who knows? Aren't they great?' Joel was stroking first one, then the other. 'Feel this, Mandy. It's not slimy like you'd think. But it's not dry either. It's kind of in-between.'

So she knelt beside him, feeling uneasy and excited at the same time.

She reached out a hand to stroke the head of the nearest dolphin. He felt firm, smooth, and smelt of fish.

'It's not warm and it's not cold. It's kind of weird!' Joel rubbed his dolphin's nose.

Her dolphin paddled his flippers to stay in one place while they made friends. He creaked a message of rapid-fire sounds, bobbing within reach. The noise made her grin. 'Hi,' she said softly. 'Is that what you're saying?'

'Can you believe this?' Joel tickled his dolphin under the chin. 'He's smiling at me!'

'Watch he doesn't spray you!'

'Who cares? I can't believe Lauren! She never even told us about these two!'

Mandy caught sight of the vet and the trainer across the other side of the small oval pool. Mel Hartley was about twenty-five years old, tall and well built. He looked like he spent a lot of time in the water with his animals. His wavy brown hair was short, his shoulders and chest were strong.

'Do you think they like it here?' Mandy asked Joel. 'You don't suppose the pool is too small?'

He shook his head. 'It's home.'

'I know. But that's what I mean. Compare it with living in the sea!' The pool sides were white and smooth, the water hygienically clean.

Joel saw what she was getting at. 'But they were probably born here. They don't know what they're missing, do they?' He'd seen plenty of dolphinariums, and none of the dolphins in them had ever looked unhappy, he told her.

'I'm not sure.' Mandy stood up and gazed down at the captive pair. 'If dolphins are as clever as Lauren says, don't you think they'd know they were being kept prisoner?' The thought bothered her more than she could say. And yet . . . Joel was right, they didn't seem sad.

Anyway, there was no more time to talk about it. Mel and Lauren had walked full circle round the training pool and come back to join them.

Mel put Mitch down at the poolside

and they watched the little otter dive into the water. Soon he was sleek and happy, darting in-between his dolphin friends.

'Good news,' Lauren told Joel and Mandy. 'We arrived at exactly the right time.'

'How come?' Joel had shrugged off Mandy's worries. 'Is it feeding-time?'

'Better,' Lauren promised. 'Mel has to get Bob and Bing ready now. There's a dolphin show in the main arena five minutes from now. Come on, let's go see!'

CHAPTER THREE

Bob and Bing sped like silent torpedoes through the tunnel from the training pool into the big arena. They surged to the surface and leapt three metres into the air in perfect unison.

'. . . Ah!' The crowd gave an enormous gasp.

As the dolphins plunged back into the water, the crowd leaned forward in their seats.

Up they came a second time, leaping and flipping backwards together, diving, twisting and jumping once more.

'Ooh! Aah!'

Water splashed over the rim of the pool. Perched on their seats in the very front row, Mandy and Joel were soaked with spray.

Then Mel Hartley appeared through a doorway at the back of the arena. He waved at the crowd. The two dolphins surged out of the water, waving their flippers. Everyone clapped and roared.

'How do they do that?' Mandy gasped, eyes out on stalks. 'He didn't even give a signal!'

'Yes he did. See the whistle in his mouth?' Lauren pointed. 'It's high pitched so we can't hear it. But a dolphin can. They have a phenomenal sense of hearing.' She sat enjoying the crowd's amazement.

And now Mel gave another command, hard on the heels of the last one. He stood at the edge of the pool, waiting for Bing and Bob to surface. They appeared and rolled on to their backs, swam the length of the pool, twisted on to their bellies and scooted along the surface, smacking their broad tails on the water and splashing up white spray.

'Wow!' There was more applause, more cries of surprise as the dolphins went through their duet.

Mel dipped his hand into a box at the water's edge and drew out two small fish. He slipped them into Bob and Bing's open mouths at the end of the sequence. They swallowed them and swam quietly to the far side of the pool.

'Their reward,' Lauren smiled.

Mandy watched them take a rest, then glanced over her shoulder at the excited crowd. The arena sloped up behind her, row after row filled with tourists in colourful T-shirts and dark glasses, and hats to keep off the sun. It formed a huge semicircle around the fifty-metre long pool, like a great sports stadium holding thousands of spectators.

'What do you think?' Joel nudged her with his elbow. 'Aren't they great?'

'Amazing!' Their timing was perfect, they obeyed every command.

And now it was time to show the crowd more tricks. Mel hoisted a bright yellow ball on the end of a wire across the water. Fixed to a pulley, it stayed six metres above the surface, swaying gently. He raised a hand to quieten the crowd. 'Bob wants to demonstrate how he plays a great game of basketball!' he announced. He pointed to a basket fixed to a board by the side of the pool. Then he signalled to one of the dolphins.

35

Mandy held her breath. Surely Bob couldn't get the ball into the basket?

The dolphin swam to a point directly under the yellow ball, then he gave a thrust of his flippers. He jumped, his streamlined body vertical; three, six metres clear. With a twist of his head, he knocked the ball with his nose. It sprang from its clip, curved through the air and fell neatly into the basket.

'Yes!' The crowd rose to its feet and roared.

'Did you see that!' Joel leapt up, speechless.

Mandy nodded. She pointed to the doorway behind Mel. A tiny dark brown figure had come trotting into view and up on to a wooden platform beside Mel. 'It's Mitch!' she whispered.

The little sea otter stood like an athlete on the winner's podium, head raised, soaking up the applause.

Bob swam up to him, rested against the side and spat a fountain of water all over the little pretender. It sent up a wave of laughter as the sea otter shook himself down and slunk off.

Then it was Bing's turn to do a

special trick.

'Bing's game is water polo!' Mel announced. He called the second dolphin across. 'He plays a pretty mean game too!'

This time it was a bright blue ball. The trainer took it from the box and spun it in his broad hand. Then he flipped it to the dolphin. Bing bobbed up to the surface and juggled it on the end of his nose, keeping it balanced as he swam along.

'No problem!' Mandy grinned.

'Pass it here, boy!' Mel ordered.

Bing shot the ball back with an accurate pass. Mel caught it, ran alongside and threw it back. Bing surged off.

'Now, pass!'

Bing did as he was told. He shot the ball sideways into the crowd. It soared over Joel and Mandy's heads. A girl four rows back jumped and caught it with both hands.

'Bad one!' Mel wagged his finger, pretending to be disappointed. Showing that his feelings were hurt, Bing went to sulk in a corner.

But the crowd was loving it. They urged the girl to throw the ball back into the pool for Bing to try again.

'Come on down!' Mel called. 'Bring the ball with you.

Shyly the girl left her seat and came down the aisle. She was about eight years old with red hair tied back into a ponytail. She told Mel that her name was Kelly.

Mel squatted beside her. 'Kelly, do you think you can help me train Bing to make a better pass?'

The little girl nodded.

'OK. Now, blow into the whistle and get him to come.'

She blew. Bing was still sulking.

'Louder,' Mel urged.

This time the dolphin answered the call. He swam close to the spot where Kelly stood.

'OK, now throw him the ball.'

She tossed it. Bing caught it easily on the end of his nose.

'Tell him to pass it back.'

'Pass it here!' she murmured. When Bing went on juggling the ball, Kelly turned to look at Mel.

'Louder. Yell at him.'

She raised her voice. 'Pass it here!'

Suddenly Bing batted the ball neatly back. Kelly caught it. But before the crowd could cheer, Bing himself beat them to it.

Jumping clear of the water, he did a victory roll, clapping his flippers together as he disappeared in a mass of bubbles. He swam underwater to join Bob at the far end of the pool.

The game had everyone calling out for more.

'They're a couple of comedians.' Lauren sat and grinned. 'What did I tell you; dolphins have a sense of humour!'

Mandy believed it. Seeing what she'd just seen, she would believe anything about dolphins. She shook her head. 'Look, here comes Mitch again!'

The sea otter was creeping back on to the winner's podium.

The audience spotted him and roared with laughter as Mel ordered him off.

'Aaah!' Mandy cried. She felt sorry for Mitch.

'Aaah, he's cute!' People nearby joined in.

Mitch paused.

'You want him to come back?' Mel called.

'Yes!' they cried.

So Mel let Mitch come back on to the podium to take the applause. He fed him with a scrap of fish from the box. Meanwhile Bob and Bing swam quietly up and down the pool.

'Watch this!' Lauren leaned sideways to tell Mandy. 'Here comes the grand finale!'

She watched as Mel slid into the water between the dolphins. They greeted him with gentle nudges before all three dived below the foaming surface. For a few seconds all was quiet.

Then an amazing thing happened. The dolphins rose smoothly to the surface only centimetres apart. And there was Mel crouched astride them, straightening until he stood upright as the dolphins cruised the length of the pool. He spread his arms wide, balancing with one foot on Bob's back, one foot on Bing's. The crowd went wild.

'More!' they cried, as Bob and Bing parted and Mel sank between them. He swam to the side and climbed out, giving the dolphins their fish reward.

They dived, then leaped to do their victory roll. On the podium, the sea otter proudly took the applause.

'More!' The crowd chanted and stamped.

But the show was over. Mel waved and picked Mitch up. They backed off towards the door, as the dolphins glided underwater, through the tunnel, out of sight.

*　　　*　　　*

'What a star!' Mandy watched Mitch swipe a fish from the pool in the special training compound behind the dolphin arena.

'Yep, he generally steals the show.' Mel Hartley was showing them round. For a moment the fish slipped and slid between the sharp claws of Mitch's webbed front paws. The otter snaffled it between his teeth and swallowed it.

'You want to take another look at the famous duo?'

'Bob and Bing?' Joel jumped at the chance. 'Can we feed them?'

'Sure. Follow me.' He led them back to the training pool with his easy, loping stride. 'How long have you got?' he asked Lauren.

'Till suppertime. I've got a volunteer standing in for me at the rescue centre.'

They went and crouched by the pool, looking for the dolphins.

'Over there.' Mandy spotted them resting close to the surface, their triangular fins cruising through the water. 'How come they move their tails like that?' she asked Lauren. One thing about seeing them close to was that she got a chance to study their powerful bodies.

'It's because of the way the muscles are attached to the spine. Dolphins are mammals, remember. They're warm blooded. Ages ago they lived on the land, then they had to adapt to the sea. Their anatomy isn't the same as fish.'

Lauren explained carefully, seeing that Mandy would gobble up any information she cared to give.

'And they breathe air?'

'Through the blowhole on the top of their heads. It's the same with all these guys, from the porpoise to the killer whale. They all belong to the same group.'

Joel frowned. 'Hey, I thought we were supposed to feed them,' he grumbled. 'Not get a science lesson!'

Mel grinned. 'That's what Bob and Bing think too. This is the special fish snack that I give them every day. The official ration is pretty strict, so I slip them a treat when no one's looking.' He winked and told them to watch.

The dolphins had swum up and circled impatiently, making the water lap over the edge of the pool.

Mandy felt it ooze through the sides of her trainers. 'How much do they eat?' she quizzed.

Mel laughed as he reached into the box for a fish and handed it to Joel. 'Another question!'

She blushed. 'Sorry, I can't help it.'

43

She was always the same when she wanted to learn about a new animal.

Joel went more for the action. He held the fish by the tail and dangled it over the water, waiting for one of the dolphins to snatch. One rose and took it, then arched back into the water in one smooth movement. 'Who was that?'

'Bing. He has more white on his belly,' Mel replied.

'So, how much do they eat?' Mandy insisted.

'Too much, according to my boss! Bing is nearly three metres long and he weighs three hundred and fifty pounds. That's a lot of dolphin to maintain. So he eats about twenty pounds of fish in one day.' Mel knelt by the pool and slapped the water with the flat of his hand. The other dolphin came swimming up to him.

'Bob doesn't look quite so big,' Mandy said.

'More like three hundred pounds.' Mel leaned over to scratch the dolphin's head. 'He's not feeling so hot right now. Are you, boy? I have to persuade him to eat.' He reached for a fish and slipped it into his mouth. 'See how he swallows it head first?'

Mandy caught a glimpse inside Bob's wide mouth and saw a set of ridged, interlocking teeth like a zip fastener. But Bob didn't chew his food. He turned the fish so it went down head first, as Mel had said.

'And they don't mind living in a dolphinarium?' Mandy let the question slip. It was on her mind all the time she watched the show; the idea that the beautiful dolphins were somehow treated like freaks.

Mel narrowed his eyes and glanced at her. 'How should I know? I never. asked them,' he said shortly. He stood up and went to fetch a fresh bucket of fish from the cool store.

Lauren raised her eyebrows at Mandy. 'Nice one, Mandy. Bob and Bing have worked with Mel for five years, since they were babies. They were born at Ibis Gardens, and lived with their mom until she died last fall.'

'Sorry.' She blushed, then sighed. 'But it's just like Mel said: we can't ask

45

them if they like it, can we?'

They stood gazing at the pair of tame dolphins swimming up and down, up and down the length of the twenty-metre pool.

'Tell you what!' Mel said, in a better mood when he came back with the fresh load of fish. 'Since Mandy here isn't so sure that my dolphins have a nice life, why not stick around and see for yourselves?'

'How do you mean, stick around?' Joel tilted his head to one side. He was hungry, and just about ready to go back to Pelican's Roost with Lauren.

'Stay over. That is, if you're not doing anything for the next couple of days.'

'And help here?' It was Mandy's turn to jump in quickly. 'Can we?' She turned to Lauren.

'I guess. They could stay in the staff quarters if Mr Boston agrees, couldn't they?'

Mel nodded. 'No problem. I just have to tell him we've got a couple of willing helpers working for nothing. He'll say yes right away.'

'Will Boston is Mel's boss,' Lauren explained. 'He owns Ibis Gardens. Most of the staff live in.'

'Where?' Mandy had only seen the tourist bit of the theme park: the enclosures for the gorillas, the compounds for the tigers and the islands in the middle of the lake where the monkeys lived.

'At the back of the park. It looks like a motel, and it's pretty basic.' Mel told them what to expect. 'No luxuries.'

'Do we get a TV?' Joel wanted to know.

Mel grinned. 'Sure. But if you stay, I'll work you so hard you won't have time to watch it!'

'How about it?' Lauren was looking at her watch. 'Do you want to phone your grandpa and ask if it's OK?'

Still Joel hesitated. 'We work for nothing?'

'I'll give you your food and board. And a whole new look at the life of a dolphin!'

'Can we help with the shows?' Joel asked. 'Will Bob and Bing perform their tricks for us?'

Mandy grew impatient. She would have said yes ages ago. Two or three days living with dolphins; feeding them, cleaning their pools, maybe even swimming with them, and definitely learning everything there was to know. Why on earth was Joel being so cagey?

'They will if they trust you,' Mel told him, looking them both in the eye. 'But if they don't like you, no way!'

This was a challenge even Joel couldn't back out of, Mandy knew.

'OK,' he agreed at last. 'Let's phone home and tell Grandpa we want to stay!'

CHAPTER FOUR

'What is it with you and the dolphins?' Mandy asked Mel. She dangled her legs over the side of the training pool, watching him teach them a new trick.

The idea was for Bob and Bing to swim side by side, with Mel in the middle. He was to give three blows on the whistle, then grab each dolphin by the nearest flipper. Then they would tow him through the water at high speed. After only two tries, they'd got the hang of it. Now they did it perfectly each time.

'I guess I don't really know.' Mel hauled himself out of the pool and sat beside her. Water streamed from his wetsuit as he leaned over to throw the dolphins two small fish. 'But it's something special. Some kind of bond that you can feel but can't put into words. I just know how lucky I am to have them trust me the way they do.'

Mandy nodded. She liked Mel, she decided. She wished she could say the same about Will Boston, the owner of Ibis Gardens, who strode towards them now. It was first thing on Sunday morning, before the park had opened.

'Hey, how's it going?' he said briskly. He carried a rolled-up newspaper which he tapped against his leg all the time he spoke.

'Hey, Will,' Mel said without looking up. He was studying Bob as the dolphin turned away from the fish he was offered.

'I was just talking to the kid, Joel.'

Mandy squinted up at the boss of Ibis Gardens. The sun had risen behind his shoulder, leaving his face in dark shadow. But she could tell from his voice that he wasn't pleased. She imagined a frown, a mouth turning down at the corners behind that bushy black moustache, and she could also tell that he and the dolphin trainer didn't get on.

'The kid says you're not happy with Bob. What's wrong? Is he sick or something?'

'I don't know yet.' The trainer stood up, hands on hips. 'He's not eating much.'

Will Boston grunted. 'He looks fine to me.'

'Yeah.' Mel stooped to sprinkle water over Bob's back as the dolphin rose to the surface for air. 'Maybe it was something he ate. Some kind of stomach bug.'

'Or maybe he's fooling you, wanting you to feel sorry for him so he doesn't have to work.' The boss made it clear he wouldn't stand any nonsense. 'These dolphins are smart; remember. But I can't afford to have one of them falling sick.'

'Yeah, yeah.' Mel had heard it all before. 'We know that, don't we, Bob? Four shows a day, six days a week. Tell Mr Boston there's no reason to worry.'

Bob creaked an answer from deep in his throat. Mandy hid a smile. It sounded for all the world as if the dolphin had understood exactly what Mel had said.

'The show's nothing with only one of them out there. We need two. That's the way we advertise it, as a double act, and right now we can't afford to rest them.'

Mandy heard Will Boston scratch the stubble on his chin as he rubbed his hand up and down his face. She'd taken a dislike to him the moment she saw him. It wasn't his stocky, short-legged figure, nor his bristling moustache. She knew other men like that without wanting to run a mile. It wasn't even his high-pitched, whiny voice. It was the dead look in his eyes as he bossed people about, that way he had of not looking directly at anyone.

Now he noticed her sitting there. 'You hear that? Don't let these guys fool you. Let them know who's boss.'

Mandy couldn't think of any reply, so she smiled foolishly instead.

'The other kid, Joel; he says you're from England?'

She nodded.

'Well, I hope you're gonna go back home and tell folks what a great place we have here at Ibis Gardens. Major attractions. "Little Africa", we call it. Why go through the hassle of the real thing when you can jump on a plane and fly right here?' He whacked the newspaper against his leg and aimed it at her like a gun. 'What do you say?'

Afraid to say anything, Mandy nodded again.

'OK, well that's great.' He glanced at his watch. 'First show of the day in half an hour. You make sure this dolphin's in good shape for me, you hear?' He altered his sights to rest on poor Bob.

'Sure thing,' Mel said in sharp response.

Mandy felt she should stand to attention as the owner of Ibis Gardens rapped out his opinions.

Will Boston was satisfied that he'd got his message across. He lowered his newspaper to his side. 'You have a nice day now,' he said as he pulled Mel to one side.

Mandy was glad to be left in peace with the dolphins. She'd spent a restless night in her room, listening to the noisy air conditioning. The bare, stuffy room had made her feel a long way from home.

But as soon as she'd got up and had breakfast of blueberry muffins and hot chocolate, she'd come out with Mel and Joel to say hi to Bob and Bing. Already she felt better. Just to see them rise to the surface to greet her, watching the water roll off their broad backs, seeing them breathe, made her feel glad to be alive.

What is it with me *and dolphins?* She changed the question she'd put to Mel a little earlier.

'Is it the way you swim?' she asked out loud. 'Or the way you always want to play?'

'You know what they say?' Joel came up suddenly from behind.

Mandy jumped. 'No, what?'

'About talking to yourself. It means you're going crazy.' He sat and dangled his bare legs in the water.

'I wasn't talking to myself, I was talking to Bob and Bing.'

'Same thing,' he shrugged.

'No, it's not,' Mandy said. 'Didn't you know that talking to dolphins can be a whole lot more enjoyable than talking to some people?' She could prove it right there and then. 'You want to see?'

Without waiting for an answer, she

took the whistle that Mel had left on the fish box and hung it round her neck. Then she jumped into the pool.

The dolphins reacted with a warm welcome, swimming up quickly and nudging her. Mandy tried not to be nervous, remembering how Mel behaved with them. For a few minutes she just swam, letting them get used to her being there.

'So?' Joel demanded. 'What am I looking at?'

'Wait.' She decided it was time to put the whistle to her lips and give three short blasts. Would it work?

Yes; Bing came alongside, and then Bob. She was in the middle. The dolphins were offering her their flippers so that she could hold on. Then they were kicking with their tails, surging along the surface, gathering speed. They towed her between them. Mandy felt the water part in a great wave, felt the splash of spray, then the gentle let down as the two dolphins came to a halt. They swam apart to let her sink deep into the clear blue water.

When she came up again, Mel was

standing beside an astonished Joel.

'Pretty good!' Mel clapped slowly. 'Let's keep it in the act!'

Out of breath, amazed that the trick had worked, she clambered out of the pool. 'What do you mean?'

'Keep it in,' he repeated. 'You did real good.'

'Me?' Mandy stared back at him. 'Do that in front of a whole crowd?' Her knees went weak at the idea.

'Sure. Why not?' Mel grinned and slapped her on the back. 'You got the dolphins on your side; now you can get them to do any trick you like!'

*   *   *

'OK, Mandy, way to go!' Joel urged.

There was a sea of faces in the arena. Mel had introduced her as his guest assistant. She stood dressed in a grey and blue wetsuit for this last show of the day.

'You OK?' he whispered.

Her legs trembled, her mouth felt dry. 'I wish I'd never agreed to this!'

Mitch the sea otter was doing his

thing of sneaking up on to the podium. The crowd roared with laughter.

'Go for it!' Joel gave Mandy a small shove so that she stood in full view of everyone. The audience spotted her and began to clap and shout.

'This girl is fabulous with animals, believe me!' Mel told them.

Mandy stared at the rows of people. It was all a blur of bright colour and noise, rising to the back of the arena. She spotted Will Boston leaning on the rail at the front, waiting nervously for her to perform, obviously pinning his hopes on her to thrill the crowd. There was no backing out now.

So she ran and dived neatly into the pool, came up and whistled for the dolphins. They came at her call, turning to have their tummies tickled and nudging against her to say hi. She stroked them, and Bing offered her his flipper. Together they paddled to the middle of the pool.

Soon Mandy found that she could ignore where she was. All she knew was that she was with the dolphins, proud to be their friend. She relaxed. The trick would go fine. Bob and Bing wouldn't let her down.

'Ready?' she asked as Bob followed them across the pool. She put the whistle to her mouth and gave the short signal, waiting for the dolphins to settle into position. Then she seized their flippers and waited for them to set off.

Their strong tails began to churn through the water, the waves parted ahead of them and they were off. Mandy held tight. They raced the length of the pool, spray flying, the cool water washing against her.

There was a cheer, and cries for Mandy to do it again. So she waited for the dolphins to turn, then gave a second signal. They towed her back down the pool in triumph.

When it was over, Mel and Joel reached out their hands and hauled her out. 'Terrific!' Mel congratulated her.

Mandy turned and took a bow, grinning as Mitch stole the limelight from the top of his platform. She heaved a deep sigh.

'I knew you could do it!' Joel was

pleased for her.

Mandy even saw Will Boston give her a thumbs-up sign, relief written all over his dark features.

'Thanks to Bob and Bing!' Mandy gasped, glad that it was over, proud that they'd done it. She remembered to dip into the box for their fish reward and patted their heads as Bing came up to feed.

'Come on, Bob!' Joel coaxed.

But the smaller dolphin was still off his food. The show continued, rolling on with the next trick, thrilling the audience. When it was over and the dolphins had made their final leap before they swam off down the tunnel, Will Boston came hurrying across.

'Great! Keep it in!' He beamed at Mandy. 'The crowd loved you! Word will get round and takings will go up! Who knows, you could help Ibis Gardens get over our small financial problem.'

Mandy blushed, promising to do it again next day.

'If Bob is up to it,' Mel reminded them. He'd unzipped his wetsuit and slung a towel around his neck. 'I'm getting concerned. He's definitely not eating enough, and he's slowing down.'

Will Boston shrugged it off. 'Quit worrying. He looks fine to me. If he was sick, he wouldn't want to do the shows.'

'Maybe. But Bob likes to please. I reckon he'd keep going even if he felt lousy.' The trainer shook his head and sighed.

'Forget it!' His boss blustered his way through. 'I want this kid to keep the trick in, OK?'

'Listen, Will, how about giving Bob a couple of days off?' Mel refused to be beaten down. 'I think he needs it.'

'No way!' came the rapid reply. 'What, and let thousands of people down?' He spread his hands, palms upwards. 'What can I do? They come to see dolphins, and dolphins is what they're gonna see!'

He turned on his heel and marched off, muttering to himself. 'Who does this guy think he is? Telling me the fish needs a break!'

'Bob isn't a fish!' Mandy protested.

'He knows it.' Mel was still shaking his head. 'All he thinks about is dollar signs; money, money, money! Come on, let's get out of here. How about I take you guys for an ice cream up at the Springs? We could all use a break, and there's just time to drive up to Dixie before sunset.'

'Great idea, thanks!' To Mandy, the idea of sitting by the bay at dusk, eating ice cream, not to mention watching for wild dolphins, was too good to be missed!

CHAPTER FIVE

The red sun was low in the sky. It cast a pink glow over the white houses of Dixie Springs, as Mandy, Joel and Mel picked their way between the rows of sponges set out along the quay.

'Can we take a boat out?' Joel asked. They'd finished their chocolate chip ice creams and were taking a stroll along the pier, looking for dolphins. There was just time to do a circuit of the bay before the sun sank out of sight.

'Sure.' Mel seemed to have his mind on other things. 'You and Mandy go. I'll wait here.'

'Is that OK?' Mandy checked. Mel still looked worried. 'You don't want to go back and find out how Bob is?'

Mel smiled. 'No, you go ahead.' He spoke to a fisherman who was pottering in his boat, and fixed up a quick trip for Mandy and Joel. 'See you!' he called. 'Watch out for those dolphins. Steve Peratinos here will take you to the best places. He keeps a log.

Ask him.'

Soon they set off, and curved across the still water towards the setting sun. Their fisherman was a friendly old man with strong, wiry arms and broad hands that gripped the wheel. He wore a faded denim cap, and his face was lined from years in the sun.

'What kind of log do you keep?' Mandy asked. Every ripple in the sea's smooth surface promised a dolphin sighting, but so far they hadn't been lucky.

'I write down how many dolphins I see, what they do, which direction they swim in. Stuff like that.' Steve Peratinos swung the boat round towards the far shore. 'We set up a Dolphin Watch last year.'

'Who's we?' Joel asked. The breeze blew through his T-shirt and against the peak of his cap, so he decided to turn it around and wear it back to front.

'Guys who fish round here. And the coastguards, a couple of scientists from Orlando . . . you know.' Steve's deep, gravelly voice drifted on. 'The best time is around spring, when they have their young. That's when the count shoots way up!'

'I guess we missed it.' Joel moved restlessly around the edge of the boat, peering down.

'Over there!' Mandy pointed to an area close to the shore. She'd spotted dolphins.

Steve altered course. 'Yeah, you missed that part,' he explained, 'but the young calves are still around. You might hit lucky.'

'We already did.' Mandy pointed again. Two dolphins had risen to the surface close by; a mother and her offspring by the look of things. 'Isn't that great?'

She saw how the calf shadowed its mother, rising for air then diving out of sight. Then there were more dolphins, weaving through the bow wave of their boat, playing in the spray. 'How old is the calf ?' she asked.

'Four months, maybe five.'

'It's quite big already.' The calf was almost as long as its mother, but much thinner.

64

'How long do they stay together?'

'Mother and calf? Let's see. The young guy won't leave her side until he's six months old. Then he'll go off to catch a few fish. But he won't be weaned until he's a year and a half old.'

'Wow! Did you see that?' Joel shot across the boat to the far side. 'Three of them jumping way out. Did you see it?'

'Sit down, you're rocking the boat!' Steve warned him, then he went on explaining to Mandy about the young calf. 'He feeds on milk, just like you and me.'

Mandy frowned. 'Underwater?'

Steve laughed. 'It's kind of neat. Mom has a slit in her belly. When she wants to feed the baby, out pops the nipple.'

'P-lease!' Joel cried, pretending to cover his ears.

Steve went on: 'And the calf's tongue kind of makes a tube when he presses it against the roof of his mouth. He puts his mouth to the nipple, Mom squirts milk into the tube, and there you go. One pretty neat system, hey?'

'Amazing!' Mandy marvelled. Another mystery solved.

'Hey!' Steve cried, as Joel ignored their conversation and flung himself back across the boat for a better view of the acrobatic dolphins. 'Steady!'

But the warning came too late. The boat rocked from Joel's reckless leap. He overbalanced and tried to catch hold of the rail.

'Grab him!' Steve yelled at Mandy. 'He's going over!'

She lunged and touched Joel's fingertips as the boat tilted and he slipped away, across the wet deck. The next second, he was gone.

Stung into action, Steve cut the engine. 'Man overboard! Can you see him?'

Over the side, down in the deep blue water, there was a froth of bubbles rising to the surface, but no sign of Joel himself. 'No! He's gone under!' cried Mandy.

The three playful dolphins gave up their game and vanished. Four or five others swam quietly nearby.

It was as if time stood still. Mandy

stared down at the rising bubbles, stunned by what had happened.

Then Steve unhitched the lifebelt and threw it into the water. 'Did he hit his head?' he yelled at Mandy.

'I don't know. It happened too quick.' She was kicking off her shoes, ready to jump into the sea. Someone had to dive down there and see.

'Hold it!' Steve was there beside her, holding on to her arm. The boat still bobbed dangerously. He didn't want a second emergency if Mandy were to leap out into danger.

She strained to get free. 'Please!' she begged. 'He could drown!'

'Wait!'

There in the blue water, from way down deep, shapes were rising.

'See!' Steve hung over the side and pointed through the surge of bubbles.

Yes; something was coming to the top, rising closer and closer. Mandy could make out wide tails, long snouts; the young dolphins bunched together lifting a pale shape between them. Joel! His body looked limp as it broke the surface.

The water drained off him as the three dolphins buoyed him up. The sudden light hit him and he moved. Mandy saw him take in a great gasp of air.

Thank heavens! Now Steve let go of her and she jumped over the side. She hooked her arm through the lifebelt and swam with it. 'Grab this!' she told a dazed Joel, swimming between the three dolphin rescuers.

He was shocked, but able to do as he was told. He struggled into the belt and flopped back, breathing deeply.

Mandy held on to him, and towed him towards the boat. Sure that he was safe, the dolphins backed away. She thanked them silently, but out loud, she told Joel off.

'What do you think you were doing?' she cried, clinging to him with one hand, and hanging on to the side of the boat with the other. She waited for Steve to haul him back on board. 'You were down there ages. We thought you'd drowned!'

'I must have blacked out.' Joel slumped across the deck, his legs dangling. 'I don't remember.'

'Lucky for you, the dolphins knew you were in trouble,' Steve told him. He helped pull Mandy to safety.

With both of them back, breathing heavily, shocked but all in one piece, they gazed out to sea.

The sun was a fiery ball on the orange horizon. Streaks of pale gold clouds streamed across the sky. The water shimmered silver. And there, criss-crossing the bay, leaping and diving, were the wonderful dolphins who had rescued Joel: a trio swimming in harmony, disappearing into the distance.

Steve nodded and turned the engine on. He told Mandy to keep an eye on Joel to make sure he didn't do any other fool thing, then he swung the boat to face the shore.

He shook his head as he thought of the narrow escape. 'That sure is one for the log!' he said.

*　　　*　　　*

'The amazing thing was, these dolphins

were completely wild,' Mandy told Lauren Young on the telephone. 'They knew nothing about us humans. Yet they realised straight away that Joel was in trouble. How?'

She was sitting with Joel in the cramped staff quarters at Ibis Gardens. Mel had insisted that they rang Jerry Logan to tell him what had happened, even though Joel said he was perfectly fine now. He'd even made him stay inside to rest.

'It's only eight o'clock,' he'd complained.

It was already dark, with a muggy feel to the air. There was no breeze and there was a thick covering of mist which had rolled in from the sea.

Anyway, here he was grounded, following his grandpa's anxious orders, and there was Lauren from the rescue centre on the other end of the line.

'How did they know he needed rescuing?' Mandy asked again.

'It's uncanny, isn't it?' Lauren agreed. 'Like they have a sixth sense. They really are the most wonderful creatures!' She checked once more that

Joel had survived the experience unscathed. Then she asked Mandy to put Mel Hartley back on the phone.

'What is this?' Joel asked. 'Why the big deal?'

'No big deal. Those three dolphins only saved your life, that's all!' Mandy pushed her hair back from her face and tried to listen in to Mel's conversation with Lauren.

'. . . Yeah, I guess you'd better come over first thing tomorrow,' Mel told her. '. . . I don't like it . . . No, our resident vet is still on vacation and I can't get hold of anyone else right now. Could you come?'

Say yes! Mandy prayed. She too was worried.

'You know what the boss here is like,' Mel went on. 'It's crazy. He won't spend money on good fish for the dolphins; he buys the cheap stuff. Sometimes I think it's no wonder Bob's gone off his food. And Boston keeps on telling me the Gardens is in financial trouble, that's why he can't afford to give the dolphins a rest.'

Mandy frowned. 'How come? That

71

doesn't make sense; the crowd for the show is always huge,' she whispered to Joel.

He shrugged. 'Don't ask me. Say, did the wild dolphins really save my life?'

'Yep.' How many times did he need to be told?

There was a pause. 'Wow!' Another pause.

Mandy strained to hear Mel.

'Boston's so tight with money I buy extra fish for Bob and Bing out of my own salary. I've been telling him he'll have to spend more ever since last fall, when we lost Dorothy, Bob and Bing's mom. Same problem; I know she got sick because of the cheap food we were giving them. Of course, the guy won't listen . . .'

'This is more serious than we thought!' Mandy listened with a knot of worry growing in her stomach. The dolphins obviously needed to be fit and happy to be able to work well in the show. 'What if the same thing starts to happen to Bing as well?'

Joel shook his head. 'Maybe we can persuade Mr Boston to get some help.'

Mandy doubted it. Expert help cost money. 'We're going to have to go behind his back,' she warned.

Obviously Mel agreed. '. . . So you'll come over?' he said to Lauren at last. 'OK, we'll see you first thing in the morning!'

*   *   *

'What do you mean, you can't do anything for him?' Will Boston was yelling at Lauren Young.

It was early on Monday morning. Lauren had driven over from the rescue centre as dawn broke. Now she stood by the dolphins' training pool in the middle of a huge row with Will Boston.

Mandy heard him shout and broke into a run. She'd woken up early, listening for Lauren's truck to drive past the staff quarters. The moment she'd heard it, she'd quickly slipped into her shorts and T-shirt and headed straight for the pool. But it seemed she'd already missed the vet's verdict on Bob.

Lauren stood her ground, folding her arms and letting the owner of the theme park finish before she answered. 'He's got a high fever,' she explained. 'He's slow and listless. And he's not been eating properly for the last few days. He's sick for sure.' She glanced apologetically at Mel, who stood next to her, arms folded, with a worried expression.

'So, what's he got?' Boston demanded.

'I can't say. I'm no dolphin expert. You need a second opinion.'

'And my vet's on vacation. I don't have the money to spend on bringing in a marine expert. Just give us a clue; what do you think it is?'

'Could be a virus. Or it could be something to do with the type of food he's getting.' She shrugged and turned back to Mel. 'How old is he?'

'Five and a half, nearly six. That's no age for a dolphin. They can live up to forty years.'

'This is crazy!' Will Boston raised his voice still further. 'I'm paying you to tell me the dolphin's got the flu?' His face was red with frustration as he thought of the problems it would cause with the daily shows.

'I didn't say that,' Lauren said calmly. 'It could be his diet, remember. I'm saying you need to bring in an expert. I know a guy from upstate, but it could take him a couple of days to get here. A lot of people call him for help. I know; I phoned him to check.'

'A couple of days?' The boss's jaw fell open. 'What are we supposed to do? Close down until your so-called expert can get here?'

She nodded. 'That's my advice.'

'No way!' he warned Mel. 'You didn't hear her say that, OK? It's a complete disaster if we have to close the show. No one pays money to come through those gates unless they know for sure they're gonna see Bob and Bing!'

Mel hung his head and muttered.

'Look, I'm doing my best here, OK!' Lauren turned away with a shake of her head. 'I'm telling you you've got a sick animal. Pretty darned sick, as a matter of fact.'

Mandy bit her lip. This was the first time anyone had admitted they were really worried about Bob, and she knew from what she'd seen at Animal Ark how quickly animals could go downhill once they fell ill. She felt her chest go tight with fear.

Even Mr Boston was stopped short. 'What are you saying? This illness; is it bad?'

Lauren spread her hands. 'I don't know. Get Matt Greenaway to come down from Orlando. He'll give you a proper diagnosis. Meanwhile, I'd say you should keep the dolphin in isolation, in case he's infectious.'

'You mean the other one could catch it too?'

'Maybe. It's best to play it safe from now on.'

'Cancel the shows?' There was a wobble in Will Boston's voice.

'For sure.' She gave her advice, rolled down her sleeves, told Mel she was sorry that there was nothing else she could do.

The trainer turned to reason with his boss. 'The fact is, Mr Boston; if Bob here gets any worse—if he isn't given time off and a chance to recover—there isn't going to *be* any Bob and Bing show ever again!'

'Don't give me that!' The plea fell on deaf ears. 'I know you dolphin people; you think the least little snuffle means the end for them. You want to pamper and spoil them, as if nothing else matters. Well, I've got a whole park to run, and it's not easy.' He turned to Lauren. 'So no more talk of isolation and cancelling the show,' he insisted. 'Let's just see how it goes!'

Mandy had heard enough. She didn't wait to say goodbye to Lauren, but went off instead to visit Bob and Bing.

The dolphins were swimming quietly at the far end of the pool. They didn't rise through the water to greet her, so she knelt and slapped the surface. Bing came up slowly, sucked in air and let himself be patted. But there was no liveliness in him this morning, no mischief. Soon he turned and dived back to the bottom to join Bob.

She sighed. 'What's wrong?' she murmured into the wavy depths.

There was silence, except for the lapping of the water against the side of the pool. Of course, a dolphin couldn't talk back. Not in any language she understood.

Then she heard the patter of webbed feet across the tiles, and here was Mitch, out of his cage, scurrying towards her. Mel followed more slowly.

'What do you want?' Mandy said to the sea otter with a smile. Tame as could be, he scrambled on to her lap.

'He wants to play,' Mel said, gazing down at the shadowy shapes of his two dolphins. 'I wish we could say the same about Bob.'

The sick dolphin rose feebly to the surface for air. He blew faintly and looked at them with weary, half-closed eyes. Then he turned heavily and dived to the bottom again.

'So do I,' Mandy sighed. She'd never wished so hard for anything in her life.

CHAPTER SIX

They separated Bob and Bing as soon as Lauren had left. She'd advised a shot of antibiotics for Bob, just in case it helped. And when she'd given him the injection, she insisted that he needed to be in a pool by himself.

'Won't they get lonely?' Mandy had asked. The two dolphins spent all their time together. If they were separated, both Bob and Bing would be sure to pine.

Lauren had admitted Mandy could be right. 'But what can we do? The last thing we want is for Bing to get sick too.' Keeping Bob in isolation was the only way.

So Mel decided to keep the sick dolphin in the smaller training area, while Bing was put into the main show pool.

'See, he doesn't want to go!' Mandy watched the trainer trying to herd Bing towards the tunnel. The dolphin would swim slowly up to it, then stubbornly turn tail and go back to Bob.

'I'm sorry.' Mel was just as determined. 'If the vet says we have to take you away from him, it's for your own good, you hear!' He tried again. Again Bing swam to the narrow entrance, then heaved up out of the water, flipped on to his back and rolled down to join Bob once more.

Mandy watched sadly. Tears came into her eyes as she watched Bing sticking faithfully by Bob's side. Poor Bob was hardly moving from the far corner of the pool, but he did seem to greet Bing with a nudge and a flip of his tail whenever the bigger dolphin returned to his side.

'You don't suppose they know best?' she murmured. 'Lauren could be wrong about Bob being infectious.'

'I can't risk it,' Mel decided. He didn't like this any more than Mandy did. 'You'd better jump into the pool with me. The two of us might be able to get him through the tunnel.'

Reluctantly Mandy dived in and swam underwater. She kicked hard, keeping her eyes open, until she reached the dolphins. Bubbles of air escaped from her nose as she twisted and came alongside Bob. She put her arm around him and stroked his nose. Feebly he flicked his tail and leaned his head against her. Bing paddled gently nearby, watching Bob's every movement, refusing to leave him.

Mandy needed air, so she kicked upwards and broke the surface.

'Bing really doesn't want to go,' she pleaded. 'He realises there's something wrong!'

'I know.' Mel got ready to dive under. 'But we can't ignore Lauren. What we'll do is both dive down and swim to either side of Bing, OK? We'll grab a flipper each to show him we mean business. He's strong enough to shake us off if he wants to, but he trusts us enough to do it our way. We keep hold of him and guide him to the tunnel. Once he's got his nose in there, we'll block his way back. That way he'll have to swim forward and we close the door after him.' He waited to see that Mandy had understood. 'Got that?'

She nodded and took a deep breath.

81

'Come on, let's do it!'

Mel disappeared below the glittering surface and Mandy followed. They kept to the plan, and when they had hold of Bing's flippers, they began to ease him away from Bob. For a few seconds Mandy expected him to resist. But though he turned his head to look back at Bob he decided to let the humans have their way. They eased him towards the tunnel, gently pushed him through head first, and at last slid the door shut behind him.

With her lungs aching, Mandy shot towards the light. Her head and shoulders burst out of the water and she gasped for air. Mel was by her side, telling her she'd done well. 'I couldn't have done that without you!'

Mandy shook her head. 'How come I feel so bad then?' She remembered that last look that Bing had given Bob. It was as if he knew he was saying goodbye for good.

'Let's take a break.' Mel swam for the side. 'I have to report to the boss.'

They climbed out together. 'I'll stay,' Mandy decided. 'Are you going to tell him we'll definitely have to cancel?'

'Yep. He'll go ballistic, but what can we do?' Mel trudged away to deliver the bad news to Will Boston. 'I'm gonna get on the phone to Matt Greenaway one more time,' he called back. 'I haven't been able to get through yet, but we need him down here just as soon as he can make it!'

He disappeared and left Mandy alone by the pool. By now the sun had risen well into the sky, but there were still deep shadows from the high wall that kept the training pool private and closed to public view. Beyond the wall she could hear visitors passing by, eager to see the elephants in their enclosure, gasping in surprise as they came across the rare mountain gorillas. A chair-lift whirred by, giving people a bird's eye view of the park. Further away, a giant water slide went into business; there were loud screams and a wild splash as the carriage hit the pool at the end of the ride. Life beyond the pool went on as normal.

Mandy sighed and leaned over the water to watch poor, sick Bob. He was swimming in slow circles, obviously looking for Bing. When he saw Mandy, he flipped his tail and rose to the surface.

'Hi!' She reached out to stroke him.

He hardly reacted. But he stayed close, taking in short bursts of air, still searching for his friend. He tilted his head towards her, as if to ask what they'd done with him.

'It's OK, he's safe in the big pool,' Mandy explained. 'We only took him away because you're sick. It won't be for long.' Her heart ached as the dolphin turned this way and that, gave a series of faint creaks, then gazed up at her again.

But Bob was so weak he could hardly move his flippers to stay afloat. His body dipped below the surface, then he struggled to rise.

And now Mandy began to be really afraid. Bob sucked in air, then sank. He rocked from side to side, unable to use his flippers to steady himself. He was sinking, then feebly trying to rise with a desperate flick of his broad tail.

Mandy stood up and looked around.

Bob needed help, and she was certain that he needed it right now.

'Mel!' she cried. She heard someone come in through the tall gate. 'Come quick!'

But it was Joel. He ran to her side. 'I just saw Mel in the office, talking to Mr Boston. What's wrong?'

'Oh, Joel, it's Bob. I think he's dying!'

He knelt to look. The dolphin could only just make it to the surface.

'If Matt Greenaway doesn't get here soon, he's going to be too late!'

'He needs air.' Joel acted quickly. He slipped into the water and tried to hold Bob up. 'Run and fetch Mel,' he called.

But Mandy couldn't leave them. 'Joel, he's saying goodbye. I know he is!'

Bob was nodding his head slowly, gasping and rolling in the water. And for all his effort, Joel was failing to hold him steady. In the end, he had to let him go.

Then the dolphin was free to float. He was making no movement, his blowhole was relaxing and letting in water. His eyes were closing for the last time.

Mandy watched the dolphin die. His lungs took in liquid. He dropped below the surface. Slowly, slowly the clear water met over his beautiful head and he sank to the bottom of the pool.

*   *   *

Mel sent word to Matt Greenaway that it was too late; Bob was dead.

'I can't believe it,' Mandy whispered to Joel. She felt crushed. 'I knew he was really sick, but I never thought he'd actually die.'

Joel stood by the side of the pool with her, watching them lift the body from the water. Bob had been so graceful, friendly and full of life. 'Me neither.'

'It's awful to think how he must have suffered.'

'Don't, Mandy. It's bad enough.' He walked away, his head hanging, unable to talk.

If only they could go back in time, just an hour, even half an hour, to when he was still alive! Mandy wished for the impossible. *Maybe I could have done something to save him!*

But it was too late. She too hung her head, and began to cry.

Lauren came and put an arm around her shoulders. 'It's tough,' she whispered. 'But we've still got work to do. I have to send samples to the lab in Orlando for tests to be done. We may never know what killed him,' she told Mandy, 'or maybe they'll find a virus. The important thing is making sure Bing stays well. Let's wait and see.'

*   *   *

It was early the following day, and everyone was slowly coming round from the shock. Outside the dolphinarium, life at Ibis Gardens still went on as usual.

'. . . So, we can go ahead with one dolphin,' Will Boston declared. 'Change the routines here and there, so that Bing takes over the tricks that Bob used to do. He can shoot a ball into a basket, can't he?

Mandy shuddered. She stared at the theme park owner. Less than twenty-four hours after Bob had died, and Mr Boston was acting as if he couldn't care less. She still felt empty inside, and stunned.

And she sensed that Bing knew what had happened too. He'd swum restlessly near the surface for hours after Bob had died and been taken away, as if he'd been calling for him, longing for a reply.

Mel stood by the training pool shaking his head. 'I can't do that to him,' he argued.

'Why not? You know what they say—the show must go on.' Boston pointed at Bing, now swimming in slow circles deep below the surface. 'We still have a solo act here. And I can ship in another couple of dolphins for you to train up to join the show in a few weeks' time. What's the problem?'

Mandy could hardly bear to listen. Instead, she slipped her hand into the fish box and tempted Bing to the surface. She petted him and tried to comfort him as the two men talked on.

'The problem is, Bing here is pretty cut up about Bob dying.'

We all are, Mandy thought.

'You can't just go on as if nothing happened,' Mel insisted. 'Dolphins aren't machines. They're complex beings with highly developed intelligence and deep feelings!' His speech came from the heart as he looked his boss straight in the eye.

Boston shrugged. 'Yeah, well don't forget they pay your salary! And mine, and everyone's on the site. The dolphin show is what keeps this theme park going!'

Mandy stroked Bing's head and whispered to Joel. 'Let's jump in and keep him company.' Together they slipped into the water to swim beside the surviving dolphin.

Mel shook his head at Boston. 'This dolphin isn't fit to do the show, OK? How can I make this any easier for you? He just lost his lifetime companion. He doesn't know what hit him. It's called grief. He's lonely. I'm not gonna ask him to perform!' His face was red with a deep anger, his voice rising.

As Mandy and Joel swam alongside Bing, they knew that every word Mel said was true. Bing came close to them for contact, and still seemed to be looking everywhere for his missing friend.

Will Boston narrowed his eyes. He took a step back, then held his own. 'Lonely!' he retorted. 'You're crazy. You're telling me a dolphin thinks like a person?' There was a sneer on his broad face as he came to squat by the side of the pool. He watched Mandy and Joel swimming with Bing.

'So he can talk and tell you how he's feeling, can he?' he taunted.

'He doesn't have to.' Mandy couldn't help answering back. 'You can tell by the way he's acting.'

'He won't eat the fish, see.' Joel tried to add his opinion to the argument. 'And he won't play. Right now he should be rolling over and swimming under us, ducking and diving, fooling around. He hasn't done any of that since yesterday.' They'd brought him back into the training pool after Bob had been taken away, and he'd carried on calling and looking for him in vain.

'He's not sick too, is he?' Will Boston went into a panic. 'You say he's lost his appetite?'

Mel nodded, ready to make a stand. 'He needs better quality fish. I already ordered it from the supplier.'

Boston gritted his teeth, but for once didn't complain. 'Has he got this fever, the same as the other one?'

'No. His temperature's normal,' Mel assured him. 'Whatever was wrong with Bob, Bing hasn't come down with it yet. It's like I said, he needs a better diet to build up his strength, especially now he's pining for his friend.'

Mr Boston stood up with the air of a man who had no more time to waste. 'So, take his mind off it, put him back to work,' he said abruptly. 'How soon can you get him ready?'

They might as well not have bothered, Mandy realised. She slipped her arm around Bing and stroked him on his nose.

Mel couldn't give any answer. He bit his lip and sighed.

'Put it this way, you've got until Friday.' Will Boston was on his way to the gate, striding off without looking back. 'Teach him the new tricks. Oh, and keep the kid in!'

From the far side of the pool Mandy glared at his disappearing back. Her eyes flashed. 'What if the kid doesn't want to stay in?' she muttered under her breath.

The gate slammed. Bing flicked his tail and dived out of sight.

'And what if the dolphin says no?' Joel said through clenched teeth.

CHAPTER SEVEN

'Bing's gone on strike,' Mandy told Jerry Logan. Joel's grandfather had driven over from Pelican's Roost to see how everyone was. It was Wednesday morning and it was growing clear that the surviving dolphin was desperately unhappy. He lurked at the bottom of the pool, refusing to do any of his tricks, coming up only for air.

'You gotta see his point of view,' Jerry admitted. 'He's already lost his mother, and now his brother. How would any of us feel if we lost someone special twice in such a short time?' With his wife, Bee, away in England he knew what it was like to feel lonely. He turned to Steve Peratinos, who'd been brought in to give his advice.

The fisherman and the Green Earth gardener were old friends. They'd both lived on Blue Bayous all their lives and cared about nature and wildlife more than the likes of Will Boston. The theme park owner was a businessman and a newcomer as far as they were concerned. So they stood at the poolside with serious faces, watching the solitary dolphin.

'Can you think of anything that would help?' Mel asked. He'd racked his brains to find ways of cheering Bing up. 'I need to get him back in action, or else I'll have my boss on my back. But Bing doesn't want to know.' He pointed to a couple of coloured balls that bobbed on the surface. The dolphin had ignored them all morning.

Steve shrugged. 'The only thing that's gonna help this guy is the passage of time,' he murmured.

'Time is what we haven't got. Will's given me till the end of the week.'

Mandy had seen the posters by the main gate: 'Dolphin Shows Four Times a Day. Resumes Friday.'

'Bad news,' Steve tutted. 'I've seen a dolphin take weeks to get over something like this. And that's out in the ocean where there's a whole school of them to help him cope.'

'Something like what?' Mandy was curious.

94

'Like, a young dolphin can lose his mother, say in an accident with a tuna net.'

'I thought they were against the law?' The big nets had been banned because of the damage they did to other sea creatures.

'Sure. But you get these big fishing companies. They think they're above the law. So once in a while, a mother dolphin gets killed. At Dolphin Watch we can put a tag on the young one and track him. You find he comes up to small boats, looking for the dead mother, maybe thinking the boat's a strange sort of dolphin; that it'll adopt him.'

Mandy sighed. 'Poor thing. So then what happens?'

'In the end he gives in and joins up with the nearest pod. But it takes him a few weeks to accept that the mother's gone. He seems to need someone special, and who can blame him?'

'Mel, *you're* special to Bing,' Mandy pointed out. It seemed strange that the dolphin had turned his back on his trainer.

He frowned. 'I thought I was,' he said slowly. 'Now I'm not so sure.' He gazed down at Bing, then at the balls floating uselessly on the surface. 'Bing did trust me, but I kind of get the idea that he thinks I let him down.' His voice fell away, dejected.

'No, you didn't!' Mandy objected. She knew Mel cared more about the dolphins than anyone else.

'I was the one to take him away from Bob when he was dying. That can't look so good to him.'

Steve stepped in to reassure him. 'He'll come round. It's too soon right now. Like I said, he needs time.'

They'd come back to where they'd started. Time, as Mel said, was what they hadn't got.

Sadly the men moved off, leaving Mandy alone with Bing. They'd tried everything: changed Bing's diet, studied the results of the lab tests and asked advice from everyone they knew. Nothing had given them a clue about what to do for the best.

'Oh Bing, what can we do?' Mandy sighed, sitting to dangle her feet in the pool. She felt the sun on her back, and could hear the hum of visitors, the whirr of the cable cars.

'I've got an idea,' a voice said out of the blue.

She turned to see Joel, his cap perched on the back of his head, his hand delving into the fish box. 'What are you doing?' She jumped up as little Mitch came scampering towards them. 'Who let him out?'

The sea otter's webbed feet flapped on the wet surface, his broad tail smacked the ground. He smelt fish.

'I did.' Joel grinned at her. 'I figure if anyone can solve Bing's problem, it's gotta be Mitch!'

The sea otter grabbed and swallowed the fish, then plunged into the water. He darted to the far side of the pool and hopped out, spied Bing and dived in again; a dark, streamlined shape swimming close to the dolphin's head, inviting him to play.

Bing let Mitch say hello, then turned away. He swam slowly down the length of the pool.

Mitch shot to the surface and

popped his broad head out of the water, his whiskers dripping, his large brown eyes puzzled. Then he disappeared for a second attempt. He raced after Bing and caught up with him, twisted underneath and came up the other side.

Joel and Mandy watched the two wavy shapes; one small and dark, the other large and shadowy. As they saw Bing ignore the sea otter's games, their hearts began to sink.

'Come on, Bing, play with Mitch!' Mandy breathed. She was on her hands and knees, craning out over the water.

Joel frowned. 'If Mitch can't help him, nothing can!'

But Bing was still too sad about Bob to take any notice of the lively little sea otter. Yet again he turned away.

Joel threw him another scrap of fish. 'Hey, look!' he whispered as the dolphin followed Mitch slowly to the surface. For a moment, they thought it had worked.

Mandy dug deep into the box for a fish to reward him with. Surely now Bing would come and feed, get over what had happened and let them coax him with treats. Mitch hopped out of the water and gave a short, pleased bark. Mandy held the fish at arm's length, tempting Bing to snatch it.

But the dolphin had only come up for oxygen. He rose like a submarine until his back broke the surface and he took in air. There was a wash of water against the side of the pool, a splash as his tail hit the surface. Then down he went, ignoring Mandy's fish, turning his back on his friends.

'No good.' Joel had to admit defeat. He scooped Mitch into his arms and stood there, head hanging, disappointed that his plan hadn't worked.

'You know what?' Mandy shook her head, recalling what Steve Peratinos had told them about dolphins getting better more quickly in the company of others. 'I think Bing is going to get so lonely here without Bob he could die!'

'No way.' Joel didn't want to hear this. He made off with Mitch, to put him back in his hutch.

Mandy ran after him. 'No, listen; he

won't eat, he won't follow Mel's signals with the whistle. What I'm saying is, he won't take an interest in anything that's going on.' She paused. They stood by the gate, looking back at the pool. Bing had dived to the bottom and the water was still.

'So? It doesn't mean he's gonna die!'

'Of a broken heart,' Mandy said quietly. 'Don't you believe in that?'

Joel looked away. 'I guess. So what are you saying?' Mitch was squirming and wriggling over his shoulder, so he walked on with him, letting Mandy follow.

'I don't know!' Her thoughts were confused. Then she went back to what the fisherman had said. 'Joel, what would happen if we put Bing back into the ocean to be with other dolphins again? You know, like Steve said about the orphan dolphins. They look to the others to help them. Bing would do the same if we gave him the chance!'

'Put him back?' Joel repeated. He stared at her as if she'd gone crazy. 'How? How do you get a great big dolphin from the middle of an amusement park to the Gulf of Mexico?'

'I don't know how!' She hadn't thought this far. 'But what do you think? Would it work?'

Joel had opened Mitch's cage and put him back inside. The sea otter scuttled up and down, then sank his broad front teeth into a gnawed branch in the corner and chewed at it. 'To set him free?' He turned to her, jamming his cap over his forehead. 'Let's get this straight. You want Mel to ask Mr Boston if he's ready to let Bing go?'

Mandy nodded.

'For nothing?'

'Yes. Why not?'

'Do you know how much this dolphin's worth?'

'No. But whatever Bing's worth in money, you can't keep him cooped up here to pine away and die!'

'Thousands of dollars. Big bucks. Boston keeps telling us Ibis Gardens is short of money, remember. He isn't going to kiss goodbye to his star attraction!'

Mandy hesitated. Even she could see

the point. 'What if we got someone to pay Mr Boston the money Bing is worth? Then he'd have to sell him.'

'Who?'

'I don't know. Lauren might have enough money at the rescue centre.'

'No way. They always need more money to look after the birds and animals they rescue.' Joel was definite about this. 'Gran works there for nothing because they can't afford to pay her.'

'OK, then; Steve Peratinos and Dolphin Watch. They might be able to buy Bing and release him.' She trailed off as Joel shook his head once again. 'OK; the Millers next door to us at Pelican's Roost. They've got loads of money.'

'Mandy!' Joel spread his hands. 'Aren't you forgetting something?'

'What?'

'Even if we could raise the money somehow, we'd still have to get Mel on our side.'

She paused. Yes, she'd been racing ahead as usual. 'OK, so it would be a hard choice for him. I know that.'

'Like, he's worked with Bing since he was born. And he's already lost Bob.' They were walking down one of the main paths through the park, against the steady flow of visitors which was filing in through the gates. 'Think how it would feel if he had to say goodbye to Bing as well.'

'Terrible,' Mandy admitted. 'But, like I say, it would be even worse if Bing stays here and pines away.'

'Who's pining away?' Mel himself came cutting through the crowd towards them. He'd just seen Steve Peratinos and Jerry Logan off and was hurrying back to the dolphinarium. 'You mean Bing, don't you? How is he?'

'Not good,' Joel admitted. He told him about Mitch's failed attempt to cheer him up.

Mel listened in silence. 'OK, and let me guess what you two were discussing.' He went and leaned on a wooden rail by the alligator compound. A couple of two-metre long specimens were lazing in the mud by the edge of the lake. One opened its wide gash of a mouth and showed them its rows of spiked teeth. 'You think we should get Bing out of here,' he said quietly.

Mandy gasped. 'How did you know?'

'Because it's pretty much what I figure too.' He was thinking hard, staring at his hands which he'd clasped together as he leaned his elbows on the rail.

The two alligators shifted into the water and sailed gently away. They looked like pieces of driftwood, except for the two pairs of gleaming yellow eyes.

'That we should set him free?' Mandy glanced at Joel with new hope.

Mel nodded. 'This latest disaster is the final straw, as far as I'm concerned. After all, what kind of life does he have here now that Bob's gone?'

From the big island in the middle of the lake, a troupe of monkeys squealed and chattered at the approach of the alligators. They swung away through the trees.

'I've been thinking things through ever since Dorothy died last year. What right do we have to keep them in the first place? OK, so it's been my life. Training dolphins to do these shows, getting them to trust me. But I guess it's time to make changes.'

Joel broke the silence. 'So what now?'

The trainer stood up straight, as if he'd made his decision. 'Go to see the boss,' he told them. 'Get him to give Bing his life back.'

'Now?' Mandy asked.

There was firmness in his stride as he made his way to the office.

'Sure. Do you want to come?'

Mandy was there with him, her chin up, determined for Bing's sake that they would make Boston see sense.

'What if he says no?' Joel demanded. He ran ahead of them and started to walk backwards, begging them to think before they acted.

The office door was open. They could see the head and shoulders of the park owner as he sat at his desk.

'Don't worry, he'll say yes,' Mel told them, without a moment's hesitation.

*   *   *

'No way, no way, no way!' Will Boston slammed his desk drawer. 'You've seen the posters! We begin again Friday!'

Mandy could feel Mel trembling with anger. She didn't know how he kept his own temper as his boss flared up.

'We can't begin unless the dolphin is willing to perform,' he pointed out.

'What is this? You're telling me you can't train this animal to do the act?' Boston raged on. 'It's a dolphin, not a movie star!' he ranted.

'Bing's got a mind of his own, and if he's not ready to do it, there's nothing I can do.'

'You call yourself an animal trainer!'

Mandy saw Boston's dark moustache quiver. He'd turned them down flat; no way was he going to let Bing go free.

'Let me make it clear. We re-open Friday with one dolphin. I'm buying two more dolphins from Underwater World up in Star Bay. I've just called them. They can send a truck down tomorrow. The dolphins are fifteen months old.'

'That's too young,' Mel cut in. 'They're not fully weaned. The guys at Underwater World should know that!'

'Tough. When they get here, you start training. I'll give you two months to work them into the show. Think you can do it?' The question came out as a sneer as he walked right up to Mel and stuck his face out in a fresh challenge.

Mel measured his reply. 'OK, so if I train two new dolphins, does that mean that at the end of two months, I can take Bing and put him in the ocean?'

If he lives that long, Mandy thought. She felt her heart thumping inside her chest, she saw Joel shaking his head and looking down at his feet.

Will Boston laughed in Mel's face. 'Nice try. But like I said; no way!'

Mel jutted out his chin. For a second, Mandy thought he was going to take a swing at his boss.

Instead, he turned and headed for the door. 'Fine. I quit!' he yelled. 'I'm out of here!'

Stunned, she watched Will Boston's mouth fall open, heard him turn and thump his desk. Then she and Joel ran after Mel as fast as they could.

*   *   *

The porch lights were on at Pelican's Roost. Jerry Logan had invited a bunch of people over for the evening. There was Lauren Young from GRROWL, Steve Peratinos from Dixie Springs, and Mel Hartley himself. It was only hours since he'd quit his job at Ibis Gardens and he was already regretting his decision.

'You did the only thing you could,' Lauren told him. She was sipping a cool drink, looking out across the garden at the white beach beyond.

'But what happens now?' Mel had left Bing in the lurch. He'd stormed out of the office and straight out of the gate. Joel had only just been able to calm him down enough to drive over to his grandfather's house to explain what had taken place. Jerry had rung round and invited the others over for the evening.

'Let's just get our heads around this,' Steve said. 'Did you quit, or did Boston fire you?'

'I quit.'

'So change your mind. Give him a call, say you want your job back.'

Mel sank his head on to his chest.

'He doesn't,' Mandy explained. 'What we all want is for Mr Boston to let Bing go. We think it's his only chance since he's so miserable without Bob.'

'Wow! I'd say we have a big problem on our hands. What do we do now?' Steve asked.

'We can't steal a dolphin from under his nose, that's for sure!' Jerry Logan tried to make light of it. He went inside for more drinks, but somehow his words stuck in Mandy's head.

"Can't steal a dolphin!" They spun around inside her brain as Jerry served pizza and salad to go with the drinks. They stuck in her mind as they finished the meal and she took the plates inside to stack them in the dishwasher. "Can't steal a dolphin?" Mandy gazed at her reflection in the dark window.

'I don't see why we can't steal a dolphin!' Mandy said to Joel as he brought more dishes into the kitchen.

'Uh-oh!' He caught the glint in her eye, the stubborn note in her voice. 'No, don't tell me!' Joel backed away, raising both hands as she came towards him.

But Mandy grabbed him before he could escape. 'Come with me. I want to tell you something!' She took him to walk on the beach under the moon and stars.

*   *   *

'. . . Steal a dolphin?' he echoed.

'We need a big tank full of seawater and a truck. One of those giant trucks you see taking oranges to the factories on the mainland. Only instead of a load of oranges, we would have Bing in the tank.' The waves rose and crashed on to the shore. Moonlight glittered on the black sea.

'. . . We'd tell Mr Boston that Bing was sick.'

'Like Bob?'

'. . . Say he'd caught the virus. Mr Boston would have to believe us if

Lauren gave him the news. She'd tell him that Bing needed to go to a dolphin clinic somewhere.'

'In Orlando?' Joel remembered that Matt Greenaway, the dolphin expert, worked there. Still he shook his head and walked barefoot along the beach. 'You're crazy!' he said.

'. . . Boston hears from Lauren that Bing needs urgent treatment. He has to let the truck come into Ibis Gardens to pick him up for the journey. Only, it's not Matt Greenaway's truck, it's us!'

'And we take him to Dixie Springs?' Joel was beginning to get the picture.

'To Steve and his Dolphin Watch people.' Mandy was so excited, she could hardly keep from running back to the house and spilling it out to the grown-ups. 'We get the tank down into the harbour and we set Bing free! He'll swim out to sea. Other dolphins will come to meet him . . !

'Mandy!' Joel warned. 'I'm not sure we should do it. I mean, we're breaking the law here!'

She nodded. 'I know. But if we don't, Bing is going to die. First his mother, then his brother. Are we prepared just to hang around and wait for it to happen to him too?' It wasn't just her; Mel thought the same way, and he was an expert.

'OK.' Joel considered it and agreed. 'But there's still a pretty big "if" in this before we even get near to putting your plan into action.'

'What?' Mandy couldn't see any flaws in her argument. And there was no time to lose. She was heading back up the beach over the soft, silvery sand.

'*If* we can get Lauren to help us,' he pointed out, running after her. 'We have to get her to tell a pretty big lie, remember!'

Mandy gulped. Joel was right. Was there any way Lauren would go along with their plan?

*   *   *

'It's a matter of life and death!' Mandy begged Lauren Young to listen to her. The grown-ups sat on the Logans' porch trying to decide what to do.

'We could go to jail for stealing.'

Joel's grandpa wanted them to steady down. 'This is pretty big stuff!'

'But what else can we do?' By now Joel was firmly on Mandy's side. He'd had time to think about it since she broke the idea to him on the beach.

It was a question that no one could answer.

'Who says Will Boston will listen to me?' Lauren asked. 'He's had this fight with Mel here, and he knows Mel and I are good friends. Even if we did try Mandy's plan, I don't think he would trust me.'

They sat in their cane chairs, staring up at the stars. For a while no one spoke.

'So, who *would* he trust?' Joel wanted to know.

There was another silence. Slowly every head in the group turned towards Mandy.

'Me?' she yelped, jumping up in surprise. This was something she hadn't bargained for.

'Sure. You heard what he said: "Keep the kid in!"' Joel insisted. 'He likes you!'

'He doesn't even know me!' All Will Boston knew was that she could do a good trick with his two dolphins. The crowd liked it, and whatever the crowd liked, Boston was in favour of.

'But you're the one who could persuade him to listen to Lauren.' Joel explained it slowly, refusing to let her back off. 'You could go in tomorrow like nothing had gone wrong, ready to work with Bing. Act all innocent!'

'Me?' Mandy was finding it hard to agree. 'But that means I'd have to be nice to Mr Boston!'

'You can do it. Think of what would happen to Bing if you don't.'

'So, she says she'll train Bing until the boss hires another helper?' Mel looked ahead. 'He says yes. She works for a couple of hours then goes back and tells him she's called Lauren to take another look at the dolphin because he's sick. That's when Lauren gives her verdict; Bing needs to go to the clinic in Orlando!'

'You got it!' Joel grinned at them. 'What do you say?'

Mandy stared at them in turn. Mel

was nodding, Jerry was talking it through with Steve Peratinos.

Even Lauren agreed she would be willing to take the risk for Bing's sake. 'But it's down to you, Mandy,' she said quietly, fixing her with her calm, dark brown eyes.

Mandy took a deep breath. Even though it was her idea, she hadn't imagined playing this major role. It would be like acting a part in a play. Could she do it?

'Mandy?' Joel grew impatient. 'We gotta decide.'

'OK,' she said at last. 'I can't make any promises that I can pull this off, but I'll give it a go.'

CHAPTER EIGHT

'Hi, Mr Boston!' Mandy breezed into the office at Ibis Gardens early next morning. Joel and Jerry Logan had driven her across and wished her luck. They would wait in the car park for a while. Then, if all was well, they would drive on to meet Lauren and Mel at GRROWL. Meanwhile, Steve Peratinos had contacted his Dolphin Watch friends and they were on standby at Dixie Springs.

Will Boston was on the phone. He was worried and cross as usual, when he looked up and spotted Mandy. 'What? Oh, hi!'

He turned away to argue down the line. 'Listen, you gotta take those two young dolphins back to Star Bay! I can't keep them here . . . I just lost my trainer, that's why! . . . No, I don't care if the truck's already set off. You call the driver and tell him I changed my mind!'

Mandy watched him slam down the

phone. She felt the palms of her hands begin to sweat.

'Whadaya-want?' he snapped.

'I came to help with Bing,' Mandy said, all sweet and bright.

Boston's frown deepened. 'You know I fired Mel Hartley?'

She held his gaze. Not so much fired, as the other way round, she knew. But she said nothing. She hoped her innocent, bright-eyed stare would settle his suspicions.

'Yeah, you were there,' he recalled. 'So how come you still want to work with the dolphin?'

'I like him,' Mandy said simply. 'And he likes me.'

Boston sniffed and twitched his moustache. 'You think you can work with him alone until I get someone else?'

'I'd like to try.' She was doing OK, keeping a smile on her face, though her hands were hot and sticky now, and her mouth felt dry.

Boston shoved papers around on his desk and snatched up the phone once more. 'Mac, is that you? Get the 'copter out for me, will-ya? I gotta go to Miami to talk to my banker.' He glanced up at Mandy. 'Go ahead, what are you waiting for?' he snapped. No thanks, no grateful smile.

So Mandy slipped out before he could change his mind.

'Just don't let Mel Hartley get the idea that he can come crawling back!' he yelled after her. 'Tell him from me never to show his face, OK! Good trainers are a dime a dozen!' He punched more numbers into the phone, too proud to admit he was wrong.

Mandy was over the first hurdle and heading for the dolphinarium. It was only eight o'clock; too early for visitors to be allowed in the park. A few keepers dressed in green polo-shirts and fawn shorts were sweeping and mucking out in the animal compounds. They gave her a friendly wave.

She hurried on, glad to find the gate to the training pool unlocked, but afraid of how Bing would be after his second lonely night. Hoping he would at least be hungry, Mandy took a bucket of the new fish from the cold store.

Normally he would have come to the surface the moment Mel had blown the whistle. But this morning, like yesterday, it was different. Mandy blew twice, then three times. She could see the dolphin's shadowy shape settled in a corner, ignoring the high-pitched sound.

If Bing wouldn't come to her, she would go to him, Mandy decided. She dived in and swam underwater, greeting him with a fond pat. He gave a small response, lifting his head to let her tickle his flat chin, as if he still wanted to please her, then he rose with her to the surface.

'That's right!' Mandy encouraged. 'See, it's not so bad up here. I've brought some beautiful fish for your breakfast.' She talked on as she swam to fetch it, thinking that the sound of her voice would boost Bing's spirits. Her own hopes rose as he followed in her wake, making low creaking noises in reply. He was 'talking back' in his own way, trying his best to be friendly.

'Nice fresh fish,' she cooed, reaching into the bucket. 'Mel ordered it specially for you.'

But Bing veered away as she dangled it in front of his nose. He wasn't hungry.

Mandy sighed, then climbed out to try a game with him. If he wouldn't eat, maybe he would play. So she brought the blue ball and tossed it into the water. It landed with a splash. 'Come on, Bing, pass it to me!' She stood at the poolside, hands outstretched, waiting for him to flip it back with his beak.

Again she was disappointed. The dolphin swam up to the ball, then straight past, nosing it out of the way in a sad, empty manner. He disappeared to the far end of the pool.

What else could she try? Other noises to attract his attention. She rattled a pole against the metal fish bucket and waited. Nothing. Bing didn't move from the deepest part of the pool. She even sang a song about sailing across the sea, sailing home, sailing to be free.

She sang the words from the bottom of her heart, willing the dolphin to shake off his grief and listen. But he'd been too badly affected by Bob's death to respond.

'Oh Bing, my singing can't be that bad!' Mandy pleaded. It hurt her to see him like this—so sad and lonely. Was this the same dolphin who had played tricks on people and fooled around to please the crowds? It was hard to believe as she peered into the pool and saw him barely moving, his face turned to the wall.

Something had to be done. It was time to put the next stage of their plan into action.

'Don't worry, we're going to get help,' Mandy promised him. She got up from her hands and knees and went to use the public phone beside the main gate. 'Lauren, can you come?' she said quickly.

'I'm on my way!' she promised. 'Give me twenty minutes.'

Just time to tell her that all was going according to plan so far. 'Mr Boston doesn't suspect a thing!' she whispered into the phone. Then she hung up and went to walk by the lake until Lauren showed up.

Mandy's nerves were stretched to breaking point as she waited. Twice she went out into the car park to see if the GRROWL truck had arrived, twice she went to phone Joel and ask him to make sure that everyone was standing by.

Then, when Lauren did make it after only fifteen minutes, they both hurried straight to Will Boston's office.

'What now?' He was already at the door, looking at his watch. When he saw Mandy and Lauren, he made it clear that he had no time to spare.

'I got Lauren to look at Bing because he wouldn't do any work with me,' Mandy explained hurriedly. 'She says now he's fallen sick too.'

'What kind of sick? Not this fever that killed the other two? That's just what we need!' Worried and angry, the boss went to the phone and gave orders. 'Mac? Where's the 'copter? I told you to get it here five minutes ago!' He clicked the switch and tore into Mandy and Lauren. 'Come on, give it to me straight. Is he gonna die?'

'Maybe.' Lauren wouldn't be definite.

So far she hadn't even had to lie, Mandy realised. Instead, she'd let Boston jump to his own conclusions.

'I got a lot of money tied up in that dolphin,' Boston reminded her. 'What can you do to save him?' As always, it was money that came first.

'He needs treatment. I can't give it to him here. I'd like to take him to Matt Greenaway in Orlando. He's the best dolphin man in the state.'

Here came the lie. Mandy watched Lauren grit her teeth and drop her gaze. Luckily Boston was too busy to notice.

'Can't you get the guy to come down here?'

'Not fast enough. You want me to go ahead?'

'How much will it cost me?'

'Not a cent.'

Lauren's promise stopped Boston in his tracks. 'You can get your rescue centre to pay for the treatment? How about the transportation?'

'The people from Dolphin Watch are going to provide a truck.'

This was true, Mandy knew. Steve Peratinos had friends who owned a big truck. And Dolphin Watch could put their hands on a suitable tank to transport Bing out of Ibis Gardens. It was all laid on.

The idea of free treatment to solve a serious situation was too much for Boston to resist. Besides, the noisy grind and whirr of a helicopter's blades sounded overhead. He considered the proposal, glanced once in Mandy's direction, then nodded his head. 'Go ahead,' he grunted.

Mandy felt her heart lurch as the helicopter landed on the pad behind the office. Its blades slowed and clattered noisily, drowning her muttered thanks.

'Let's go!' Lauren yelled above the machine's roar.

As Will Boston jammed his hat on his head, ducked low to avoid the wind from the blades and clambered aboard his private helicopter, Mandy and

Lauren went into the next stage of the plan.

*   *   *

Getting Bing out of Ibis Gardens went like clockwork. Steve Peratinos was at the gate with the truck before half past nine. Jerry Logan and Joel sat in the high cab with him, ready to help lower the crate containing the special tank to take the dolphin away.

Mandy and Lauren had already dealt with the other Ibis Gardens keepers, telling them the same story that Lauren had told Will. So the gate opened for the truck and it drove slowly in.

Mandy ran alongside as it chugged towards the dolphinarium. She gave Joel a thumbs-up sign. So far, so good.

'Mel's here!' he mouthed down at her, pointing to the sleeping-compartment above his head. 'Just in case we need him.'

'Don't let anyone see him!' The news that he'd quit had spread like wildfire. He mustn't be spotted now.

But Mandy was glad Mel was there

when they finally backed the truck up to the gates of the training pool and he could get out of the cab without being seen. As Steve and the others got the tank into position and began to lower it into the pool with a pulley and chains, she spoke anxiously to him.

'I don't know how we're going to persuade Bing to do this,' she admitted. 'I can't get him to obey any orders at all. You'll have to see if you can!'

Mel nodded. He took a look into the pool. 'Poor guy, he must wonder what's going on here.'

The plastic tank had hit the water with a splash. Beneath the ripples and broken surface they could see Bing huddled in a corner.

'If you can get him to come up and say hi, I'll get ready with a shot of tranquilliser,' Lauren told them. 'He'll still be conscious and breathing, but it'll make the journey easier for him if he's sedated.'

'*If* I can get him to say hi!' Mel looked unhappy. He took a whistle from his pocket and blew a familiar signal. 'He's not gonna forgive me for this!'

Mandy watched Bing hear the sound and suddenly flick his tail so that he was pointing upwards. He seemed to be looking for Mel, waiting for another signal.

The trainer blew again and the dolphin came swimming slowly to the surface.

'He'll forgive you when he realises why you're doing it,' Mandy reminded him. It was hard when an animal trusted you and it looked as if you were letting him down.

She could hardly bear to look as Bing broke the surface and spotted Mel. He rattled out a message and rolled in the water, almost like his old self.

'Hi, Bing!' Mel reached out to him. 'Did you think I'd gone and left you on your own?'

The dolphin was too busy greeting Mel to notice Lauren come alongside with her syringe full of tranquilliser. But he felt the jab. Too late, he turned away. The drug took rapid effect and within seconds Bing was wallowing weakly in the water.

'Let's go!' The vet gave the order.

Mel, Mandy and Joel jumped into the pool. They got underneath Bing and supported him as the men in the truck manoeuvred the tank by pulling levers inside the cab. Slowly they edged it into position.

Then, when the time was right, Mel, Joel and Mandy nudged Bing into the tank. He was too dazed to resist, so Mel could give the signal for the tank to be lifted with the dolphin inside it.

Mandy saw the tank move skywards. The chains took the strain of a tank full of water and dolphin. A metal arm swung the load sideways. Soon it was lodged firmly on the back of the huge truck.

And before they knew it, Steve had slotted the crate into place around it. He and Jerry Logan made everything secure, then climbed into the cab.

'Everyone stand clear!' Jerry yelled, ordering Mel and Joel back into the truck.

Lauren nodded at Mandy. 'You did a

good job.'

'Thanks, but it's not over yet. Tell me that when we get Bing to Dixie Springs!' Mandy ran for the car with Lauren. 'Come on, let's lead the way!'

The truck was on the move with its live cargo. No one suspected a thing.

CHAPTER NINE

Mandy sat next to Lauren as they drove out of the main gates at Ibis Gardens. On the road behind, towering over them, Steve Peratinos was at the wheel of the gleaming silver truck.

They had got Bing clear of the theme park. Now they took the north road to Dixie Springs. Mandy heaved a sigh of relief and signalled to Joel, who sat between his grandfather and Steve in the cab. Behind them, tucked away in the sleeping-compartment, Mel was once more in hiding.

Joel waved back.

They were on the move; it was really happening. They were going to take the lonely dolphin to the sea and set him free! Mandy grinned at Lauren, then hung on to the rollbar as the truck braked for a posse of cyclists heading for a nearby beach. Their striped towels were strapped to their bikes, they wore beach bags across their shoulders, and they were in no hurry to get out of the way.

'Come on!' Lauren tapped the steering-wheel.

As the road cleared, she put her foot down and they were off again, past ranch-style luxury homes overlooking the beach, across white bridges built over the narrow straits. The road ran on concrete pillars over the deep blue sea. To either side Mandy could see small fishing boats and leisure cruisers, while straight ahead the road ran smooth and broad. Looking over her shoulder, she could see Bing's truck following without trouble.

'That marina over there is Captiva Harbour.' Lauren pointed out a cluster of white buildings next to a small harbour. 'The next one up is Dixie!'

After the bridge, the road curved inland. They drove between tall palm trees with graceful, feathery leaves, through patches of shade where mangrove trees grew in salt water swamps. Mandy held on to the bar as the truck swayed and the road took a curve back towards the sea. The water sparkled in the sunlight, and there, across the next bay, was the sponge fishing village of Dixie Springs.

Bing was only minutes away from freedom when Lauren picked up her car phone to answer a call. Mandy saw her stiffen as she listened to the voice on the end of the line.

'It's Will Boston!' she whispered. 'He says he's coming after us!' She slammed down the phone and gripped the wheel. Ahead of them lay a bridge across the final bay.

'How come?' Mandy leaned out of the window and strained to see what was coming up behind the truck.

'Not by road—by 'copter!' Lauren told her. 'He was on his way to Miami and he phoned Matt Greenaway to ask him if he knew whether Bing was safely on his way.'

'Oh no!' Mandy felt her stomach churn. 'And Matt told him he knew nothing about it?'

Lauren nodded. 'Right. Boston's gone crazy. He must have guessed what we were trying to do. He's been calling everyone to get hold of my mobile number and now he's managed to find out where we are and is heading back this way!'

Mandy looked up into the blue sky. There was only a jet flying high above the earth, streaming its white trail of exhaust. No helicopter, not yet. But she thought she could hear something above the roar of the truck's engine as it trundled close behind them on to the bridge. The sound was harsh and mechanical. And then she saw a helicopter lurch into view.

'What are we going to do?' Mandy's hair streamed back from her face in the wind as she craned to see.

Lauren didn't answer. She kept her foot on the accelerator and got on the phone to Steve. Looking over her shoulder, Mandy saw him pick his phone up and speak into it, and saw Joel's reaction as he heard the news. She watched him shoot his head out of the window to catch sight of the helicopter, and saw his face go pale as he turned to look at her.

Mandy still hung out of the window. The sound of the helicopter's blades grew louder. The machine was catching up, hovering almost overhead. 'What now?' she yelled above the roar.

'Keep going!' Joel cried back. 'We can still do it!' She read his lips. 'Joel says, keep going,' she gasped at Lauren. At least they all knew that Boston was on their trail. There was no mistaking it now. Above their heads, the helicopter dipped and rocked unsteadily, its blades slicing through the air as it tried to move in even closer. Through the glass dome of the cockpit Mandy could see two figures. The one at the controls must be Boston's driver, Mac, while Boston himself was leaning forward and waving his arms at them.

'Doesn't he know that his 'copter will scare Bing half to death?' Lauren frowned. Its shadow fell across the tank on the back of the truck. The noise and the sight would terrify the already frightened dolphin.

'He doesn't care.' In Mandy's mind, Will Boston cared much more about money than he did about animals. He pretended to do what was best, but he was too worried about his business being in debt to really look after them. 'He wants Bing back and he doesn't care how he does it!'

'We're never gonna shake him off,' Lauren told Mandy. She was driving as fast as she dared, keeping an eye on the overhead mirror to make sure that the truck could keep up with her. But however fast she went, the helicopter still lurched overhead. Other cars on the bridge were braking and pulling into the side of the road to watch the chase.

Then Boston came back on the phone. This time Mandy picked it up. She heard him yell at them to stop, throwing threats around about what he would do.

'If you're doing what I think you're doing and planning to put that dolphin back in the sea, I'll sue you all! That Rescue Centre won't have a cent to its name when I'm through! This is theft, plain and simple!'

'Listen, Mr Boston,' Mandy pleaded. 'Just listen for a moment!'

'Like heck I will! You tell Jerry Logan I'll wipe him out. I'll take him to court and ruin him and his gardening business! *And* that Dolphin Watch!'

'But Bing will die if you keep him at Ibis Gardens!' Mandy grabbed the bar as Lauren swung off the bridge on to a narrow road signposted to Dixie Springs. Behind them, the nearside wheels of the huge truck left the road and churned up a thick cloud of sandy soil. After a few seconds Steve got control again and managed to follow. Mandy could see that up in the cab Mel Hartley had come out of hiding and was hanging on to the back of Joel's seat.

'I said stop!' The cloud of dust rose and swirled around the helicopter as Boston carried on shouting.

'Forget it,' Lauren muttered to Mandy, her hands still gripping the wheel. 'He's not gonna listen to reason.'

So Mandy switched the phone off. The rising cloud of dust had given her a faint hope that they could keep the helicopter at bay while they went ahead with their plan. She explained a new idea to Lauren. 'Don't drive down to the harbour. That's where the road goes right down to the water, isn't it?'

Lauren braked and nodded. 'For trailers to take boats down.'

'Right. So we lead the truck away from that ramp and along the beach instead.'

'What for?' Lauren had to make a decision. Whichever way she went, the truck would follow.

'Because by driving along the beach, the wheels of the truck will churn up all the dry sand, like that soil at the side of the road back there!' She waited for Lauren to understand. 'We'll make a kind of sand storm, so the helicopter can't follow us!'

'Good thinking!' Lauren made up her mind and swerved away from the small quay. Instead, she led Steve across a patch of spiky, rough grass that led on to the beach itself. 'If we can keep them at a distance and force them to land away from where we stop, we might have time to lower the tank and get Bing safely into the water!'

Mandy hung on tight. Over her shoulder she could see the four of

137

them in the cab wondering whether they should follow. She nodded and waved them on, praying that they would understand.

'Are they coming?' Lauren's wheels had hit the beach and begun to churn up dust. She struggled to get a grip.

'Yep.' Mandy turned to face the front. Ahead lay a long stretch of empty white sand. 'This has got to work!' she muttered. She hoped that the beach would be firm enough to let them drive, yet loose enough for the wheels to kick up the dust cloud. 'Yes!' she cried, as Lauren's wheels bit and they moved on.

Now for Steve's truck. Its giant wheels sank into the sand, its engine whined, the wheels began to spin. Then the thick tread on the tyres took hold. Slowly it inched its way on to the beach.

Above their heads, the helicopter whirled in small circles. It clung like a giant insect to their backs, until the huge truck sent up a gritty cloud of dry sand. As it rose towards them, the pilot clutched at the controls and suddenly veered away, rising higher into the sky, waiting for the cloud to settle.

'It's working!' Mandy told Lauren. 'Let's go!' The faster they drove, the bigger the sandstorm. She waved Steve on towards the shoreline.

But they only had minutes. Soon Mac would rise above the dusty barrier. He might decide to steer around it and approach from the other side. Or he could land at a safe distance. Meanwhile, they had to unload the tank and set Bing free.

So they raced along the beach until the churning storm of dry sand had risen and blocked out the tiny, clean houses at the harbourside. Now, though they could hear Boston's helicopter, it was hidden from view.

'How about now? Should we try?' Lauren asked.

Mandy nodded, then hung on as she swung towards the white waves at the edge of the clear sea. Once more Steve followed.

They reached the waves and drove in, axle-deep. Then they jumped to the ground and ran to help the others slide the tank into position so that it could be lowered on a hydraulic lift at the tail of the truck. They worked in a haze of gritty sand that had begun to settle as soon as the trucks had come to a standstill.

'Make it go faster!' Joel called to Steve, as the platform lowered the tank slowly into the shallow waves.

'This is as fast as it goes!' he cried back.

Somewhere, not too far away, the helicopter hovered; heard but hidden from view.

'That's good!' Mandy whispered, keeping her fingers crossed. For as long as the dust cloud stayed in the air, they could keep Boston guessing.

At last the tank hit the ground with a thump. Water splashed and spilled over the edges, as Mandy, Joel and Mel waded into the sea up to their knees.

'Did you hear that?' Jerry Logan called from dry land. He stood with one hand to his forehead, shielding his eyes from the flying sand. 'The 'copter's landed!'

Mandy paused to listen. It was true;

the noisy engine had cut out, the blades whirred and slowed. 'How do we open this thing?' she urged Mel.

It was still impossible to see beyond the cloud, but they could be sure that Will Boston had landed some distance away, had clambered to the ground, and at this very minute was running as fast as he could towards them.

Mel showed them how to unbolt a sealed, sliding gate at one end of the tank. Inside, through the opaque plastic sides, they could make out Bing's shadowy shape. He was alert, nosing at the sides of the tank, already over the effects of the mild tranquilliser.

'When we slide this, the water rushes out and the dolphin comes with it,' Mel warned. 'Ready?'

Mandy swallowed hard. There was a band of fear around her chest, making it difficult to breathe. The helicopter blades had finally died and left a huge silence. Then there were footsteps, thudding along the sand, splashing into the shallow waves at the water's edge.

'OK!' she gasped.

Mel unlocked the final bolt. They shoved the gate aside . . . and Bing slid into the sea on a torrent of released water.

CHAPTER TEN

'Swim!' Mandy cried. She stood knee deep in the sea, urging him on.

The dolphin lay on the shore. A wave rolled and crashed against him.

'Quickly, before Mr Boston gets here!'

His footsteps came splashing along the shore. He was shouting at them to stop.

Bing was stranded in shallow water, helpless.

'We've got to get him in deeper!' There was panic in Mandy's voice. Bing thrashed with his tail, seeming to recognise what was happening. Could he hear some high-pitched signals from fellow dolphins further out to sea? Their plan was so near to success, yet so far away.

Meanwhile, Boston fought his way through the soft, wet sand towards them. 'Come on, Mac. We gotta stop this fool thing!'

Mandy could see his stooped figure

emerging through the dust. 'Bing!' she pleaded. She ran deeper into the sea, urging him on. A strong wave broke against her, almost knocking her off her feet.

Bing tried to follow. Water washed around him, almost lifting his belly clear of the sloping beach. But as the wave crashed and ebbed, he was left struggling on dry land again.

'Next time we get a big wave, we'll lift him and let him float out on it!' Mandy cried. She had one hand on Bing's broad back, one under his belly, ready to act.

Joel ran round to the far side, kicking up water, stumbling in the drag of the current. 'Come on!' He urged the next wave to swell and crash against the shore.

'No, you don't!' Boston lunged towards them, followed by his helicopter pilot.

Jerry Logan stepped into his path. 'I'll handle this,' he told Steve and Lauren. 'You help the kids.' So they came and helped Joel and Mandy to take the dolphin's weight, laying gentle hands on him as they saw the next swelling wave, the first fringe of white foam as it began to break.

'Wait!' Mandy wanted the moment to be right. 'OK, Bing, when we lift you, you've got to swim!'

The salt air filled his lungs. He scented freedom.

'Watch this!' Jerry refused to let Boston pass. The theme park boss tried to dodge sideways, but it was too late.

The wave broke with a crash. The force of the water lifted Bing, and five pairs of helping hands guided him out of danger, into deep water.

'Swim!' Mandy and Joel whispered together. They launched him gently, praying for him to use his flippers and powerful tail.

'There you go!' Mel stood up straight. 'We've done all we can. It's down to you.'

Would Bing seize his chance?

His head went back. He was listening. Time seemed to stand still as he heard the dolphins of Dixie Springs call from the wild.

Mandy couldn't see them or hear

them, but she knew they were there.

Bing glanced back at Mel. He half wanted to stay. But the lure of the deep was too strong. With a flick of his tail he launched himself out to sea.

'Fabulous!' Joel sighed.

Bing was swimming, pushing through the foam with strong strokes. Mandy swam alongside him, urging him on.

And there, gathered close to the shore, was a whole school of dolphins waiting for Bing. Sunlight glistened on the sea, breaking the surface into a million golden ripples.

Mandy felt Bing break away from her. He answered the wild dolphins, then vanished below the water.

'Goodbye!' she said out loud. A stream of bubbles burst around her as Bing dived.

She thought it was over: Will Boston standing with Jerry Logan on the beach, watching his dolphin strike out into the ocean, Mel, Steve, Joel and Lauren bunched together on the shoreline, the wild dolphins calling.

But then the most amazing thing happened. Mandy felt the water swirl

146

under her, found herself lifted from below. Her arms shot into the air as she struggled for balance, then she knew she was astride Bing. He was rising to the surface with her on his back. He was carrying her out to sea!

For a split second Mandy was scared. What if he took her way out into the deep? He was speeding out of the bay towards his new friends, who came to swim alongside them, leaping and tumbling in welcome. How would she ever get back to the shore?

She heard Joel shout and Mel whistle. But no: now she wasn't frightened. Bing wouldn't harm her. She sat safely astride his back, her arms raised in joy and delight as they sped through the water. She was riding a dolphin. It was exciting, thrilling, brilliant . . . magical!

*   *   *

Bing swept across the bay with Mandy on his back. He brought her full-circle towards the shore.

It was over. This was really goodbye.

Gently he let her down a few metres from her friends. He left her floating in shallow water and swam away again to join the school of wild dolphins. She didn't want to watch him swim away this last time. Knowing that he was safe was enough.

So she swam until her feet touched the bottom, then she waded out of the water. Tears mixed with the salt sea on her wet cheeks, as Lauren came towards her and put her arms around her.

'He's happy,' the vet whispered.

'So am I.' Mandy wiped her face. She looked up at Joel and smiled.

He nodded and grinned back.

'Listen,' Jerry Logan told them, beckoning them all on to dry land. 'Will's just had a great idea!'

Will? Mandy pulled a face. Why wasn't Mr Boston yelling at them for letting Bing go? Why was he standing there with a new look on his face? Was that a smile beneath his dark moustache?

'Tell them!' Joel's grandfather encouraged him.

They gathered round under the h
sun.

'It came to me when I saw that tric
you just did!' he told Mandy.

'That was no . . . trick!' That was on
hundred per cent Bing saying than!
you for giving him his freedom. She
was about to explain to Boston when
Joel dug his elbow into her arm.

'Great! Really great. So I'm standing
here watching the trick, and it hits me:
a unique new dolphin experience for
visitors to Ibis Gardens!' Boston puffed
out his chest, waited for them to see
the point.

'What is it?' Mel asked. 'This unique
new experience?'

'Don't you get it? We advertise a
half-day trip, setting off by bus from
Ibis Gardens to Dixie Springs. We send
them out in boats to see the dolphins.
We get an expert like Steve or Mel to
be the guide!' He spread his palms
wide. 'We go one better than showing
them dolphins in captivity. We show
them "Dolphins in the Deep"!'

*   *   *

'Whose idea was it, really?' Mandy asked Jerry.

The group of rescuers stood at the quayside after Will Boston and his pilot had flown off in the helicopter to begin making firm plans for their 'Dolphins in the Deep' experience.

The sun was already sinking low in the afternoon sky. With luck, the school of dolphins would come back into the bay at dusk and they might be able to see how Bing had settled in.

Joel's grandfather grinned. 'Let's just say I helped him to see green instead of red!'

'Will Boston's gone Green!' Mel shook his head and laughed. 'I never figured him as a friend of the earth!'

'Or of the sea,' Lauren agreed. 'But who's complaining, if it means no more dolphin shows at Ibis Gardens?'

'He plans to convert the pools into a bigger area for the alligators,' Steve told them, his arms resting on the harbour rail as he gazed out to sea. 'The biggest and the best 'gator park in Florida!'

'He never misses a chance,' Mel told them. He and Steve had agreed to help run Boston's new scheme, though they warned him they couldn't guarantee that visitors would see a spectacular ride like the one Bing had given Mandy every time they took out a boat load of tourists.

'So everyone's happy?' Jerry checked with Joel and Mandy.

They nodded.

'I guess we'll miss Bing,' Joel admitted. 'But it sure feels good to help him get his freedom.'

Mandy nodded and pointed out to sea.

In the distance a school of dolphins had broken the surface. They played and lazed in the setting sun.

'Can you see him?' Eagerly Joel scanned the horizon, hoping for proof that their dolphin had safely joined the others.

Mandy felt the warmth of the sun on her face. She shaded her eyes with both hands. 'There!' she pointed.

A shiny, sleek dolphin broke the surface apart from the main school. He leaped clear of the water in a fountain of bright water drops. He rolled as he arched through the air, flicking his tail and waving his flippers.

'It is; it's Bing!' Joel waved as the dolphin hit the water and dived down.

'I'd know him anywhere,' Mandy murmured. 'He was saying goodbye!'

And now, out there in the crystal-clear depths, Bing would learn what it meant to be free. 'It's the best feeling in the world,' she said quietly. 'It always is.'